Trouble Times Three . . .

"What's the matter with you, hoss?" Longarm chuckled. "See a mouse?" Duke was looking around warily, lifting first one hoof and then the next, fidgeting. Longarm bit the end off a nickel cheroot . . .

Something tore into Longarm's upper arm with a sudden, searing, tooth-gnashing pain . . . throwing the lawman back inside the cave portal. He dropped the cigar and clawed at the entrance timbers, but raked them only with his fingertips before hitting the ground.

The crack of the rifle that had shot him echoed demonically around the canyon. Duke screamed. Shod hooves thundered as the horse galloped out of the cut.

Cradling his wounded arm and snarling furiously—bushwhacked again!—Longarm rolled to his left as three more bullets, fired almost simultaneously, pelted the door frame and the floor just inside the entrance.

"You're dead, lawdog—y'hear?" someone hollered. "*Dead!*"

DON'T MISS THESE
ALL-ACTION WESTERN SERIES
FROM THE BERKLEY PUBLISHING GROUP

THE GUNSMITH by J. R. Roberts
   Clint Adams was a legend among lawmen, outlaws, and
   ladies. They called him . . . the Gunsmith.

LONGARM by Tabor Evans
   The popular long-running series about Deputy U.S.
   Marshal Custis Long—his life, his loves, his fight for
   justice.

SLOCUM by Jake Logan
   Today's longest-running action Western. John Slocum
   rides a deadly trail of hot blood and cold steel.

BUSHWHACKERS by B. J. Lanagan
   An action-packed series by the creators of Longarm! The
   rousing adventures of the most brutal gang of cutthroats
   ever assembled—Quantrill's Raiders.

DIAMONDBACK by Guy Brewer
   Dex Yancey is Diamondback, a Southern gentleman
   turned con man when his brother cheats him out of the
   family fortune. Ladies love him. Gamblers hate him. But
   nobody pulls one over on Dex . . .

WILDGUN by Jack Hanson
   The blazing adventures of mountain man Will Barlow—
   from the creators of Longarm!

TEXAS TRACKER by Tom Calhoun
   J.T. Law: the most relentless—and dangerous—manhunter
   in all Texas. Where sheriffs and posses fail, he's the best
   man to bring in the most vicious outlaws—for a price.

→•→ TABOR EVANS ←•←

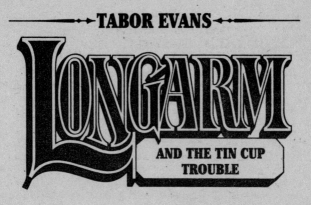

LONGARM

AND THE TIN CUP TROUBLE

J

JOVE BOOKS, NEW YORK

THE BERKLEY PUBLISHING GROUP
Published by the Penguin Group
Penguin Group (USA) Inc.
375 Hudson Street, New York, New York 10014, USA
Penguin Group (Canada), 90 Eglinton Avenue East, Suite 700, Toronto, Ontario M4P 2Y3, Canada
(a division of Pearson Penguin Canada Inc.)
Penguin Books Ltd., 80 Strand, London WC2R 0RL, England
Penguin Group Ireland, 25 St. Stephen's Green, Dublin 2, Ireland (a division of Penguin Books Ltd.)
Penguin Group (Australia), 250 Camberwell Road, Camberwell, Victoria 3124, Australia
(a division of Pearson Australia Group Pty. Ltd.)
Penguin Books India Pvt. Ltd., 11 Community Centre, Panchsheel Park, New Delhi—110 017, India
Penguin Group (NZ), 67 Apollo Drive, Rosedale, North Shore 0632, New Zealand
(a division of Pearson New Zealand Ltd.)
Penguin Books (South Africa) (Pty.) Ltd., 24 Sturdee Avenue, Rosebank, Johannesburg 2196,
South Africa

Penguin Books Ltd., Registered Offices: 80 Strand, London WC2R 0RL, England

This is a work of fiction. Names, characters, places, and incidents either are the product of the author's imagination or are used fictitiously, and any resemblance to actual persons, living or dead, business establishments, events, or locales is entirely coincidental.

LONGARM AND THE TIN CUP TROUBLE

A Jove Book / published by arrangement with the author

PRINTING HISTORY
Jove edition / May 2009

ISBN: 978-0-515-14627-1

JOVE®
Jove Books are published by The Berkley Publishing Group,
a division of Penguin Group (USA) Inc.,
375 Hudson Street, New York, New York 10014.
JOVE® is a registered trademark of Penguin Group (USA) Inc.
The "J" design is a trademark of Penguin Group (USA) Inc.

PRINTED IN THE UNITED STATES OF AMERICA

10 9 8 7 6 5 4 3 2 1

Chapter 1

Stepping down from the Burlington Flier at seven o'clock on a cool, late May evening at Denver's bustling Union Station, Deputy United States Marshal Custis Parker Long, known to friend and foe as Longarm, felt as rickety as a stove-up old grizzly fresh from hibernation on the chill slopes of Long's Peak, haunted by wintry dreams and itchy in all the hard-to-scratch places.

With a weary, involuntary groan, Longarm hefted his Winchester rifle in the same hand with which he clutched his war bag, nearly empty of trail supplies after an assignment chasing a renegade Indian agent and his whiskey-peddling kin in the Indian Nations. The tall, mustached lawman balanced his saddlebags and his McClellan cavalry saddle on his left shoulder, and paused amongst the milling crowd—arriving passengers and those jubilantly greeting them—to dig a nickel cheroot from his shirt pocket with a semifree thumb.

Ah, shit. Ah, hell. Clamping the cheroot between his teeth, he dug around in the same shirt pocket for a lucifer, coming up with only lint and a few grains of Oklahoma trail dust. He was out of matches.

"Pardon me, amigo," he said to the nearest gent. "Can I bother ya fer a light?"

The man looked over the blond head of a pretty young woman who had her arms around his neck, her face buried in his chest while cooing, "Oh, Homer, it's *soooo* good to have you home!"

Homer looked at Longarm with annoyance in his bespectacled eyes, muttering, "Of course, of course." The young man, who looked every inch the salesman—probably stationery or liver tonic—in his checked suit and shabby brown bowler, held the young woman in one hand while he dug around in his coat pocket with the other. When he had a match burning, he held it up to Longarm's cheroot with a nettled scowl.

"Much obliged, amigo," Longarm said, puffing smoke and glancing at the blonde still burying her head in Homer's skinny chest while a little boy and an even littler girl tugged at the drummer's coat sleeves yelling, "Daddy! Daddy! Did you bring candy?"

Longarm smiled at the little folks, both cuter than speckled pups.

As the crowd thinned, the lawman stood smoking and watching Homer and his young family stroll away toward a waiting hack, the little boy lugging Homer's valise in both little hands. Homer carried the little girl on one shoulder while Homer's pretty wife rested her head on the drummer's other shoulder, one arm curved around his waist, and all four dwindled into the cool evening shadows bleeding down from the peaks of the Front Range looming in the west.

"What's the matter, Custis?"

Longarm glanced over to see his porter friend, Jedediah Steele, pull up beside him and stare in the same direction with a scowl on the man's florid, gray-mustached face.

"What makes you think anything's wrong, Jed?"

"'Cause you been standing here for nigh on fifteen minutes in the very same spot, watchin' that family gather the drummer's bags like you thought you knew 'em from somewheres." Jedediah grinned slyly as he glanced up at the taller man. "You take a few too many shots of that Maryland rye of yourn, didja?"

Longarm turned to the man, an annoyed frown beetling his heavy cinnamon brows set above deep-set brown eyes flanking a tanned, sun-weathered nose with a slight bulge at the bridge that betrayed several breaks from the fists of wanted men. "How do you know I don't know 'em?"

"Well, do ya?"

"You're meddlesome."

"What's got your neck in a hump?"

"You!"

"You're cranky. Why don't you go on to your digs and throw down for a spell." Jed adjusted the leather bill of his porter's cap, hefted the clipboard in his hand, and stalked off toward the hulking granite depot. "Jeesh!"

"Jeesh yourself!" Longarm grunted after the man. Glancing around and noting that the fieldstone platform was now nearly cleared of passengers and greeters, leaving only him and a couple of cowboys and soldiers smoking and chatting desultorily around some baggage carts, he added to himself, "A man can't even stand around a train platform on his birthday and contemplate things without getting dressed down for it!"

Longarm frowned. Slowly, he lifted the cheroot to his lips and took another pensive puff.

He'd be damned. It was indeed his birthday.

For some reason he'd only been half conscious of it. It was sort of like a stone in your boot you only vaguely notice because you don't want to take the time to wrestle your boot off and shake it out. But it was there nonetheless. And if you didn't address it sooner or later, the vexing thing would likely carve a hole in your sock and grind into your foot, giving you a nettling ache and a slight limp for the next two, three days.

He didn't want to think about how old he was. He'd been at this job of hunting owlhoots every which way across the frontier for a damn long time. And now, staring hard at that figurative rock in his boot, he realized that his birthday was what had been making him feel foul all day long—from the moment he'd awakened in the club car at the western edge of Kansas, facedown on a poker table, a half-empty glass of Maryland rye in his fist, to now, standing thinking about good old Homer and his loving family here to greet him and tell him how much they'd missed him, and feeling as though the very tip of a rusty pigsticker was probing around in Longarm's chest.

"Shit," he said with a chuckle, taking another puff, "you're getting maudlin, old son. You're only a day older than you were yesterday."

As he walked across the platform and through the echoing train station, he couldn't help noticing again all the travelers being greeted by folks cooing around them and brushing off their coat lapels and pecking their cheeks and telling them they needed to fatten themselves up a little. And in turn, he couldn't dodge that lonely feeling he hardly ever felt, but that now racked him like a punch from the mouth of a darkened alley.

Damn disconcerting. It made him feel old and tired and lonesome for what he'd never had and probably never would have—a wife and a family, folks to come greet him at train stations and tell him he'd been getting too much sun and he needed to eat more or he'd blow away on the first stiff breeze. But Custis Long had made his bed long ago, when he'd decided that badge toting and marrying and settling down didn't mesh. Especially when the badge toting came with one hell of a roving eye that kept him from settling on just one woman . . .

No, sir, Longarm couldn't have seen himself trudging through life with just one gal. Life was give-and-take, and here he was on his birthday, feeling sorry for himself because he hadn't had his cake and eaten it, too.

You're a sorry son of a bitch, Longarm. You've had one hell of a good life, and here you are feeling all mopey because it's your birthday and no one knows or cares enough to give you so much as a pat on the back. And there's no family here to meet you at the train station and take you home to a supper with all the fixings including a big slice of birthday cake slathered in fresh-whipped cream. As if you deserved all that in spite of the rogue's life you chose to live a long time ago—wandering to one boudoir after another and staying out as late as you wanted, when you weren't riding the frontier chasing a badman with government paper on his head.

Free as a damn tumbleweed and as oversexed as a maverick Brahma bull fucking his way across the Texas *brasada* country as though to populate a whole new bloodline.

Boo-hoo-hoo. Poor Longarm. No birthday cake tonight.

As he headed up Sixteeth Street from Union Station, he found that castigating himself for his boyish mooning only added guilt to the lonely, empty feeling. True, he'd made his bed and it was better than most, but damnit, can't a man have regrets on occasion?

Here it was his birthday, and even though in the past he'd hardly even noted the date except in bemused passing, this one seemed important somehow—he wasn't a young maverick anymore after all—and was it so damn awful that he'd like to have someone know about it and maybe help him salute it with a nightcap if not make him a birthday cake?

He stopped at a saloon he frequented occasionally on his way home from Union Station, and ordered whiskey and beer, hoping to nudge himself out of this tailspin of a lousy damn mood, thinking of all the roads he hadn't taken instead of all those he had, and feeling sorry for himself because, as was bound to happen, here he was alone and getting old. Try as he might to smoke and drink and pick himself up, the faces around him all looked like laughing death masks, and the beer and the shot of Maryland rye went down like sour milk. A couple of old acquaintances stopped by to invite him to a game of cards, but he saw only a mocking, specterlike strangeness in their faces.

Shaking his head and mashing out his third cheroot

of the evening, he gathered his rifle, his nearly empty war bag, his saddlebags and saddle, and headed home through the dark streets in which the smoky, spicy smells of home-cooked suppers lingered as the first stars kindled and the neighborhood children were called home for baths and bed.

Like a mountaineer on the last leg of a long, hard climb, the tall, broad-shouldered lawman in the snuff brown hat and whipcord trousers clomped up the outside stairs of his rented digs to the loft above a crisp frame house on the poor side of Cherry Creek. It was good dark, and crickets were chirping. Through a couple of thinly curtained windows, he could see his elderly fellow tenants sitting around his landlady's crisp parlor playing whist or checkers while the withered and gray-haired Mrs. Pugh played the piano—some depressing, off-key hymn like "We Shall Gather at the River," or "The Old Rugged Cross," while the landlady's cat slept on the afghan-covered rocking chair nearby.

Christ.

With his thumb, he pried open his screen door, and froze. The match he always wedged between the inside door and the frame had fallen away, nowhere in immediate sight. Quickly but quietly, he propped open the screen door with his sheathed Winchester, reached across his flat belly for the double-action Colt Lightning holstered for the cross-draw on his left hip, and rocked the hammer back.

He waited, staring at the white-painted door panels, listening for movement inside. When you'd been a lawman as long as Longarm had, there were more than a few miffed cusses—either men he'd put away or family or friends of men he'd put away—looking to perforate his hide with piping-hot lead. Most of such pipsqueaks had tried to turn him toe down from ambush, too yellow to meet him face-to-face. A couple had even ambushed him from his own flat, and from his privy!

Thus, the precautionary match stick wedged in his door.

A stiff wind might have dislodged the lucifer. Possibly his landlady, Mrs. Barksdale, had knocked it out, but the persnickety old bat hadn't cleaned his rooms since his last all-night poker party with some of the old scrubs he caroused with on occasion—porters, sawyers, pimps, freighters, fallen women, and such.

Holding the cocked .44 straight out from his belly, Longarm placed his hand on the inside doorknob. The unlatched door squawked as it slid slightly open.

He had a visitor, all right. Even if Mrs. Barksdale had braved his rooms enough to clean them, she would have latched and locked the door afterward.

Hardening his jaws and tightening his grip on his .44, Longarm threw the door wide and stepped inside.

He eased the pressure on the gun's curved trigger when a sleepy female voice said, "Happy birthday, Custis."

Chapter 2

"Cynthia?" Longarm said, squinting into the room's murky shadows toward his bed.

The outside door opened into his bedroom. The small, pantry-sized kitchen was just beyond it. He could have afforded better digs even on government pay, but why shell out the extra dinero when most of his time was spent on the trail and in cheap hotels?

"What time is it?" the girl said, a shadow sitting up in the bed. His eyes were adjusting, and he saw her lift a hand to throw a thick wing of chocolate hair behind her head. "I've been waiting since five. You said you'd be getting in around five."

Longarm chuckled. "What the hell are you doing here?"

"It's your birthday," the girl said in a sleepy voice, but sounding as though he'd asked another in a long string of fool questions.

The big, rugged lawman was astounded, and his heart was shedding its shackles and rising in his chest. "How did you . . . how did you know?"

The daughter of General William H. Larimer, founding father of Denver, gave a soft little grunt as she squirmed her way up out of the bed and, shaking her long, thick mane of hair back once more, padded across the walnut floor barefoot, to stop before the lawman who was staring at her incredulously. "You told me," she said. Like a cat stretching, she placed her hands on her shoulders, rose up on her bare toes, and kissed him gently on the lips, then caressed the back of his neck with her delicate fingers. "Months ago. Don't you remember? We were lying around Uncle's rose garden, doing what we both do best, when I asked you when you were born."

"Don't remember, but . . ."

"I did. We Larimers have good heads for figures, don't ya know?"

Longarm dropped his eyes to the silky, lacy, incredibly low-cut nightgown that exposed more of her than it covered. Probably new, and probably bought in some San Francisco boutique for this very occasion. He feasted his eyes on the full, china white breasts pushing up from the flimsy garment, which, he absently estimated, would have fit in his mouth wadded up against his right cheek with room left for chewing. The Larimers not only had good heads for figures, but damn good figures. At least, the general's gorgeous, sexy daughter did—the most delectable, willowy, pale-skinned, high-busted figure he'd ever witnessed . . . and he'd witnessed considerably more than his share.

He was about to make a comment to that effect, but before he could work his suddenly heavy tongue around the words, she massaged his neck once more and said in her raspy, smoky voice, "Why don't you finish bringing in your things, Deputy? I've a bath waiting for you . . . and other things, which I'll let you ruminate on while I scrub your big, filthy carcass from head . . . to toe."

Longarm damn near shuddered with delight, but a question pressed at him. "How did you get in here? Mrs. Barksdale's the only other person with a key, and . . ."

"Mrs. Barksdale is a lovely woman," Cynthia said, running her fingers gently, soothingly in semicircles under his collar. "And she's just delighted that your sister has come to try to steer you from your devilish ways, to give you a little culture and try to put the leash on your wild streak. She's so delighted, in fact, that after our tea and pound cake, she gave me the key to your room—even heated water for your bath, which is probably ice-cold by now!—with her blessing, though she warned me that I had my work cut out for me."

"Damn, you're good."

"Aren't I?"

As he hustled his possibles in from outside, he asked her when she'd gotten back to Denver, and learned that the globe-trotting little vixen, born with a silver spoon in her pretty, bee-stung mouth, and living on dividends from her moneyed family's ample stocks and bonds and the interest from multiple, hefty, domestic as well as foreign bank accounts, had been "springing" in Antwerp with her art crowd friends, but made sure, after enjoying a lovely couple of symphonies in Vienna, that she was back in Denver for Longarm's birthday.

"Cynthia," Longarm said when she had a couple of candles burning and, shoving him down on the bed, knelt before him to pull off his low-heeled cavalry boots, "I . . . don't know what to say."

Somehow, he wanted to convey to her some of what he'd been feeling earlier, but before he could figure out a way to express it, she'd pulled his whipcord trousers and long underwear bottoms down his long, muscular legs, and was brushing her smooth cheek against the side of his fully engorged, throbbing cock and whispering, "Believe me, Custis, the pleasure is all mine."

She kissed the head of the ax-handle-hard organ gently, just barely touching it with those red bee-stung lips and sending exquisite tremors all through him. "I love the Europeans for their conversation, their class, their culture. But for good old-fashioned, Katy-bar-the-door fucking, Custis, no one can hold a candle to you."

She caressed his thighs with her long, delicate fingers and gazed up at him, her cobalt blue eyes flashing in the guttering candlelight, chocolate hair swirling across her shoulders. "Now, hop in that tub and let's get you cleaned up for the party."

"On one condition," he croaked. His heart thudded in his temples.

Cynthia arched a thin, black brow. "And what is that, Master Longarm?"

"Shed the nightgown."

The corners of the vixen's mouth rose slightly. Pushing off his knees, she stood. "That can be arranged."

Slowly, she lifted the garment so that the bottom of it slid with devastating slowness upward to expose the silky black nest between her thighs. Then it revealed her belly—flat and so china-white that Longarm thought he could see the tiny blue veins just beneath the surface of her skin. Inching ever higher, the nearly weightless gown crawled up the swollen, white globes of her breasts to rake across the pebbled pink nibbles, catching on them slightly before rising still higher until it swept her hair out from her head.

She dropped the gown on the floor at her slender feet. The thick tresses of her hair avalanched down and across her shoulders, several strands wisping about the sides of the tender long-sloping breasts and belly.

"Any more orders?"

Longarm swallowed the log in his throat and winced against the hardness in his shaft. "That oughta do it . . . fer now."

The tub's cold water did nothing to quell his desire. Cynthia bathed him with devastating slowness, scrubbing his hair and his face and the back of his neck and behind his ears before dropping into his lower regions. She worked down there even more slowly than up above, taking special care with his aching hard shaft and his balls, till he was gripping the sides of the tub in both clenched fists, before she moved down his legs to his feet.

Her breasts jostled over the sudsy water as she worked, as did the thick cascades of her hair. Her nipples jutted like thimbles, and her eyes were heavy-lidded and smoky. She cooed to him like a mother bathing her child, and he reached out once to finger a nipple, but she slapped his hand away with her sponge.

"Bad boy, Custis!"

He almost exploded right then and there, but he said the alphabet backward until she'd rinsed and dried him, dropping to both knees in front of him and drying the back of his legs while she nuzzled his throbbing cock. He grunted and groaned—no amount of Apache torture

could be more agonizing than this!—shifting his feet
around desperately to keep from losing his balance.

Finally, she tossed the towel onto a chair. She looked
coyly up at him and slid her hand up the side of his cock
from its base. Continuing to hold his gaze with a mock-
innocent one of her own, she closed her lips over the
swollen mushroom head of his shaft, moving her head
back and forth as she sucked him like a lollipop. When
she finished toying with him, he felt her warm wet lips
slide down nearly his entire length, and heard a soft
gagging sound as the head of his cock reached the back
of her mouth and started the slow plunge toward her
throat. Her expanding and contracting throat tickled him
beyond endurance, and setting his feet and thrusting
slightly forward, digging his big hands into her hair, he
gritted his teeth and sighed.

His load shot down her throat in spasming flows.

She groaned and leaned toward him, taking every
drop as she cupped his balls in one hand while pressing
the other against his rump.

It didn't take her long to arouse him again with hands
and lips and snatch. Soon he had her down on the bed on
her back, her knees raised nearly back to her ears, her
legs draped across his arms, as he thrust into her like a
mustang stallion with the springtime craze.

"Oh, Jesus—oh, God—oh, Jesus!" she cried.

"Shhh." Longarm grunted as he thrust, propped on
his bulging arms and rising onto his toes for the best
possible angle with which to drive his filly home.

"Oh! Jesus Christ!"

"Shut up, sis," he rasped, sweat dribbling down his
cheeks, his belly slapping hers. He leaned down to fill

his mouth with one of her ripe, jiggling breasts. "Mrs. Barksdale's . . . gonna think somethin' . . . downright *unnatural* is happenin' up here!"

"Oh, Jesus God, Custis . . . it *is*!"

Longarm's mood had taken a 180-degree turn by the time he awoke the next morning, spooned against the back and lovely curving rump of Miss Cynthia Larimer, his face buried in her hair, which always smelled like lilacs. Last night had been the best birthday he'd ever had—not only because of the unfettered, raging carnality that they both just barely held to a low roar—thank God, Mrs. Pugh had been in the piano-playing mood until after midnight!—but because Cynthia had remembered. Had, in fact, sailed the high seas to be in Denver for the Big Day.

How many pretty blond wives did that for their Homers' birthdays?

When Cynthia felt his dong carousing down around her delectable bottom and silkily furred snatch, she rolled toward him with a groan, keeping her eyes closed but smiling seductively, spreading her legs, wrapping her arms around his neck, and closing her mouth over his.

Thus, Longarm's birthday spilled into the early morning of the next day, as the buttery Colorado light angled through the lawman's three windows, the smell of flapjacks wafted up from Mrs. Barksdale's kitchen, and Mrs. Pugh could be heard, squeakily cooing to the Barksdale cat.

Around nine o'clock, after two more bouts of lei-surely lovemaking, Longarm rolled out of bed, lit a cigar, and stretched as he blew smoke through the angling sunlight. "Well, I s'pose . . ." he said.

"Surely, you're not working the day after your birthday," Cynthia said, her voice husky from sleep and lovemaking. "Custis, you should have a day off."

"I best make an appearance, I reckon. Billy doesn't believe in letting his deputies have a day off on the lee side of an assignment—no matter how woolly the assignment was and how many saddle galls they acquired traipsing around the Indian Nations. He won't send me out again right away, though. Probably give me some light chores around the Federal Building, playing nursemaid to some judge or such."

"Oh, Custis," Cynthia complained, resting her head on her arm as she ran her hand down his back. "I was hoping we could . . . oh . . . did you get the envelope?"

Longarm glanced over his shoulder at the naked girl on the rumpled sheets, her hair sprayed across her pillow. "What envelope?"

"It was tacked to your door when I came in. I set it on that heap of sticks you call a dresser." Cynthia yawned and ground her cheek into her pillow. "I hope it's not bad news."

"Envelope tacked to my door. Shit." That usually meant a note from his office.

Longarm stuck the cigar in his teeth with dread, and heaved himself up from the bed, his chestnut hair standing in rooster tails all around his head as he padded to his dresser. The small manila envelope shared the dresser's scarred surface with a spare .36-caliber pistol, a couple of .44 shells, a can of gun oil, a comb, and a short grocery list scrawled on the back of a wanted dodger. On the envelope, the lawman's name was scrawled in black ink, in the large sloppy hand of his supervisor, Chief Marshal Billy Vail.

Longarm sighed as, clamping the cigar between his teeth, he ripped into the envelope and pulled out the single folded leaf, which the letterhead at the top announced was "From the Desk of Chief Marshal William Vail, Federal Building, Denver, Colorado." The note itself was standard Billy, scratched in Billy's childlike hand with big looping letters: "Get in here first thing in the morning pronto." A thick, squiggly line ran from beneath the one-sentence missive to the bottom of the page, like smoke trailing an Apache fire arrow.

Longarm tossed the note onto the dresser. Not good news at all. Sounded like Billy had something more pressing for him than merely watching the bathroom door while some corpulent judge took a piss or diddled his secretary.

Longarm looked over his shoulder. Cynthia had fallen back asleep, belly down, one knee bent forward, a china white breast bulging out from beneath her chest. Her breathing was soft, deep, and regular. Born to high society, the girl hardly ever woke before noon, and then only to a long, leisurely breakfast in bed.

Longarm went over, sat down, and planted a kiss on her incredible ass. "Well, it was fun while it lasted, sugar. See you next time you're in town." He chuckled and rubbed the girl's smooth rump as she slept. "I'd bet silver cartwheels to stale doughnuts ole Homer never came home to anything like this on his birthday."

Chapter 3

"How's it hangin', Henry?" Longarm said as he pushed into Chief Marshal Billy Vail's outer office from the Federal Building's marble-floored hall, and tossed his snuff brown hat on the tree abutting a long varnished waiting bench beneath a ticking clock with large black Roman numerals.

The bespectacled, persnickety little gent in armbands—the chief marshal's secretary—stopped playing his typewriter facing the wall to Longarm's left, and swung around in his swivel chair with a disapproving sniff as he extended his hand toward Longarm while haughtily avoiding the deputy's eyes. "Assignment report and vouchers, please. The marshal's waiting, and he's not happy. You're ninety minutes late."

Longarm tossed the manila envelope stuffed full with his latest travel vouchers onto the secretary's neat, polished desk, and strode toward the door around the desk's other side. "You need some sun, Henry. You still have your winter pallor."

Pulling the vouchers from the envelope and continuing to keep his haughty gaze averted from Longarm, who always delighted in arousing Henry's disapproval, the secretary chirped, "Like I said, Deputy, the boss is waiting . . . and he isn't happy."

"When's he ever happy?" Longarm knocked once on the door, marked in gold leaf lettering CHIEF MARSHAL WILLIAM VAIL across the frosted upper pane, and pushed the door open.

Immediately, the high-backed swivel chair sitting behind the wagon-sized desk, which was cluttered with all manner of office mess, swung around to face forward. Billy Vail—short and balding and wearing a wrinkled white shirt and string tie with little silver daisies at the ends, shirt and tie no doubt gifts from his wife—gritted his teeth and stared up at the senior deputy U.S. marshal from beneath his sandy gray brows.

He didn't say anything. He merely tapped ashes from a fat stogie with more force than necessary.

"Pronto is vague, Chief," Longarm said, holding up his hands palms out. "Pronto on the night after I'd gotten in late from a long assignment could mean anywhere from nine o'clock to noon. I decided to split the difference."

"Your train was due at four-thirty."

"It got in at seven."

"That gave you roughly twelve hours of beauty sleep. If you slept at all. The messenger fella I sent over with the note told me he was dead certain he'd seen General Larimer's pretty niece being helped down from a big, leather hack in front of your place just as he was leaving. He stopped for a minute to stare in disbelief at the fine little filly climbing the outside steps to your smelly stable. As she came back down after finding your door locked, he got a good enough look at her to know for certain it was her. The man runs errands occasionally for the general himself."

"Your messenger's eyes must be bad, Chief." Longarm chuckled as he angled the red Moroccan visitor's chair comfortably toward the marshal's desk, and dropped into it. "Imagine Cynthia Larimer visiting an old sot like me in my flat. You sure you caught that messenger fella when he was sober?"

Billy Vail leaned forward, planted an elbow on his desk, and pointed his half-smoked stogie at his deputy while narrowing his eyes with castigation. "You and that girl keep fucking like a couple of muskrats up high in the springtime Rockies, the general's gonna find out and he's either gonna make me can your sorry ass or have you gelded. Possibly both. He thinks you're escorting Miss Cynthia around Denver—when the little miss deems it her pleasure to bless us with a visit, that is—to hold Denver's clamoring barbarians at bay, and also because he's under the ludicrous delusion that you and her share similar cultural appetites!"

Billy laughed and puffed the stogie, his pale, fleshy face coloring slightly.

He said, "May the Lord Jesus help you when he finds out that Thoroughbred in his barn has been rutting with a scrub mustang from the high and rocky and that that mustang has about as much appreciation for the Denver Opera as I have for a burning sack of dog shit!"

"I appreciate your concern for my welfare, Billy, but do you think you could tell me why you got me in here *pronto* on the morning after returning from a long, prickly assignment in the Injun Nations? If there's a judge around here that needs a button sewn on his fly, I'd as soon do it and get it over with."

"Sorry, no feather-duster duty, Custis." The chief marshal rolled the stogie in his lips with his fingers, the agate ring on his pinky flashing in the bright morning light angling through the window to his left. "Trouble in Tin Cup, Colorado Territory. Up high above Durango and a growing little ranching and mining hub called Gunnison."

"I know it," Longarm growled, stifling a shiver as he imagined the cold nights at that altitude this time of the year. "Hell, the snow's probably not even off those mountains yet."

"Likely not. That's why the little narrow-gauge railroad that connects Pueblo with Gunnison and about a thousand little mining camps between recommends their passengers carry shovels." Vail chuckled, pleased with himself. "In case the tracks are buried."

"You're just amusing the boots right off my feet this morning, Billy. What trouble could there possibly be up in that high country this time of the year? Those miners and high-altitude cattlemen hibernate with the bears, don't they? Aren't they all still snoring or at least sitting around their cabins playing High Five?"

"You'd think so, but you'd be wrong. The Tin Cup trouble involves the widow of a man who robbed a stagecoach thereabouts last summer versus the town itself. The man was called 'Tin Cup' Pete Duchaine, and he was one of the first men in the area. Before the upstanding citizens of Tin Cup hanged ole Pete—he shot the shotgun messenger in the process of robbing the stage—they tried to get him to to tell them where he'd hid the money." Billy shook his head as he knocked more ashes from his stogie. "No dice. It seems the man robbed that stage as a desperate act to keep the bank from reclaiming his ranch, because he hadn't been able to make the payments of late. Some recent hard winters killed nearly his entire herd. He wanted the money to go to his widow."

"So the money's buried around there somewhere," Longarm said. "And the Tin Cup folks think Pete's widow has it."

"Something like that."

"Why doesn't the sheriff or whatever lawman they got up thataway get a warrant to search her property?"

"Jesus Christ, did all that wick dipping you did with Miss Prissy Pants petrify your brain? Of course the law searched her property. Came up with nothing. Then, as of a few weeks ago, he was following a lead as to the stolen loot's whereabouts, and ended up with a bad case of lead poisoning. He's now pushing up pussy willows in the Tin Cup boneyard. His deputy"—Billy leaned forward and lifted his glasses as he stared down at a notepad on his desk—"one Chester M. Dobie, wired my office requesting help. According to him, there's holy hell to pave up there, with nearly the whole town putting away their picks and shovels to scrounge those mountains for the loot, and getting into some near-fatal dust-ups in the process. Meanwhile, the dead thief's widow has been holding men off from her ranch headquarters with a rifle. She shot one for trespassing and . . ."

"Since he was trespassing, there's nothing the deputy could do about it."

"Give the man a cigar." Vail blew thick blue smoke puffs around his head as he shuffled through some papers on the right side of his desk, scowling. "Now, I don't have time to go into all the details. Your train pulls out in exactly one hour. But I've scribbled out some notes and the names of your contacts in Tin Cup. It'll take your train three, four days to get to Gunnison this time of year, so you'll have plenty of time to bone up en route."

Finding the package he was looking for, he tossed it to the other side of his desk.

"Well, shit, Billy," Longarm said, none too happy about being sent out on assignment so soon after the last one, and even less happy about the cold country to which he was headed, "can you at least tell me what the hell business this Tin Cup trouble is of ours? Ain't this a city or county affair?"

Vail steepled his fingers beneath his chin and raised his washed-out blue eyes toward the ceiling as if in prayer. "When a city, county, or territorial official requests the help of the federal authorities, at such time that said official requests it, professing the requesting official's inability to solve the matter himself or themselves forthwith and noting that the welfare of his jurisdiction has been gravely compromised, federal law enforcement agents are duly obligated under Statute 13 of the Colorado Code of State and Federal Authority to answer that request to the best of our abilities and to uphold the local laws fully and to the totality of their letter while doing so without compromise to federal statutes."

"You been doin' some book larnin', Billy?"

Vail tapped the open tome sitting on a stack of books and papers to his right. The tome was twice as thick as most Bibles Longarm had seen, and the print on the two open pages was small enough to require a heavy magnifying glass to be read.

Longarm loosed a deep breath. "So, because the deputy asked for federal help, we have to give it."

"Pack warm socks. You'll need them as you scour the country for the stolen stage loot. And watch your back. There are plenty of others after that strongbox, and they're armed and greedy. When you find it, return it to the stage line and tell them Tin Cup folks to pull their horns in. Also, try to root out the marshal's killer, and turn him over to the deputy . . . if he hasn't been killed or run out of the country by the time you get there. Before you leave there, you might also need to orchestrate a local election to seat a new marshal."

Billy rocked back and forth in his swivel chair, scratching the back of his head and smiling like the coyote that ate the pet prairie dog. "Oh, and . . . I'll expect a full report upon your return as always."

Longarm blinked slowly, staring across the desk at his boss. This sounded like a job better suited to an entire cavalry troop than just one man. But there was no point in arguing or asking for backup. He knew Billy too well.

First, Longarm would investigate. Afterward, if he found the trouble too much for one lonely badge toter, he'd wire for help. But then, and only then, would he get it . . . if there was help to be had, that is.

Longarm chuckled wryly and shrugged a shoulder. "Well, if that's all, Billy—hell, I'll be on my way. If I leave now, I should be back by Christmas."

"Look at it this way. I'm sending you because you're the only deputy I have who has one shot in three dozen of settling things down up there."

"Now you got me blushing." Longarm scowled down at the large manila envelope across the front of which Vail had penciled "THE TIN CUP TROUBLE." He folded the envelope once and stuffed it into his shirt pocket beneath his black frock coat and summer-weight fawn vest, then turned toward the door. "You're a hard man, Billy."

"Not near hard enough."

"Hard enough . . . sendin' a feller all the way over to the western slope the day after his—"

"Oh, Custis . . ."

Longarm stopped with one hand on the doorknob, and turned back to Billy Vail, who was grinning at him through the smoke cloud wafting around his round, balding head.

"What now?" the deputy grunted. "You want me to clean up General Grant's lingering mess in Washington?"

"Happy belated birthday!"

Chapter 4

Two nights later and two thousand feet higher, Longarm gave his cold, limp dick a jerk, then tucked it back in his pants, bending his knees and wincing with the effort of buttoning his fly with near-frozen fingers.

The night here in Hope Creek, the little gold camp at which the High Flier had been severely grounded due to deep snow a half mile up the narrow-gauge mountain tracks, was colder than the hinges of Hell a thousand years before the Devil moved in and started the first fire.

Or so it felt to a man who'd gotten used to springtime in the lower climes.

The cold wind made the single-seater privy creak and whine as it whistled through the gaps between the boards and through the half-moon carved in the door.

Longarm pulled his deerskin mittens on over his leather gloves, turned his big frame in the tight quarters, flipped the locking nail from its hasp, and shoved the door open. The icy wind caught it and slammed it back against the privy with the sound of a pistol bark. Wood splinters fell from the door frame above Longarm's

head, peppering his hat, which was tied to his head with
a scarf knotted beneath his chin.

The lawman frowned as he glanced up, only beginning to wonder where the splinters had come from,
when a red flash appeared in the darkness ahead and left,
near the base of an outside staircase. The crack sounded
a full second later. At the same time, something blazed a
stinging line across his cheek, careened through the
privy's open door, and thumped through the back wall
behind him.

Longarm dove. He hit the frozen, wood-chip-littered
ground on a shoulder, and rolled twice before rising to
his knees. Crouching, tearing off his right glove and
mitten, he lifted his head over the top of one of the many
stacks of split stove wood forming a maze of sorts behind the saloon in which he'd been swilling cheap whiskey to melt the ice in his veins.

Again, the gun flashed near the base of the staircase.

Longarm ducked behind the woodpile as a bullet
slammed into a log before him with a sharp *whack!* dis-
lodging a couple of logs from the top of the pile while
peppering his head with bits of flying bark. Longarm
flung his glove aside, reached under his buckskin
mackinaw for his double-action .44, and rocked the icy
hammer back, instantly numbing his thumb as he lifted
up for another look over the woodpile. Two shadows ran
across the camp's narrow main street in which several
dirty snowbanks lingered, lit by the saloon's blazing
windows. The shadows disappeared between two dark
cabins.

Longarm cursed, crawled over the woodpile, and,
holding his cocked Colt, sprinted past the saloon, from

which guitar and piano music fought against the howling wind, and into the main street. He leaped a long, slender snowdrift fronting a closed and boarded-up blacksmith shop, and rammed one shoulder against the shop's front wall as he edged a cautious look down the side where the two bushwhacking shadows had fled.

"Yellow-bellied sons o' bitches," he growled, scouring the inky darkness between cabins.

He took a deep breath and bolted forward.

Trash and dirty snow littered the gap. He did his best to watch his footing by starlight while keeping an eye ahead, expecting another gun flash. Where he was, they'd have him dead to rights, but he'd be damned if he'd let the privy-shooting scum get away to try again later. He'd have his hand sawed off first, with the .44 still clutched in his frozen fingers.

He continued out the back of the gap, waving his Colt around, and dropped to a knee behind a trash pile. Ahead, a narrow path wandered between cabins and mine claims cluttered with tipple frames and Long Toms and showing in the stars blazing like fireworks in the clean, cold-scoured, high-altitude sky. Two slender shadows trotted off down the path. One of the bushwhackers said something. The other laughed.

Gritting his teeth, Longarm extended his Colt half out from his belly. With his gloved left hand, he fanned the hammer. The .44 leaped and roared until the echoes of the six shots chased each other around the cabins and barns.

When the echoes died, a man groaned beneath the howling wind.

Longarm thumbed open his Colt's loading gate and, turning the cylinder, shook out the spent brass. Striding ahead, keeping his eyes on the trail, he pinched fresh shells from his cartridge belt and thumbed them into the chambers. When the last chamber was filled, he spun the cylinder, cocked the weapon, and paused between a tipple standing tall against the stars and a small barn with a steeply peaked roof.

The barn's small door, left of the closed double doors, slapped against its frame with wooden thuds. He aimed his Colt at the door. He hadn't heard that sound a minute ago. Someone must have slipped inside.

A sharp grunt and the scrape and thud of stumbling steps sounded back the way he'd come. He whipped around to see a silhouette jostling against the blazing lights of the dance hall and saloon showing through the gap between cabins. The man took halting, running steps, limping deeply on his right leg.

Again, the barn door slapped against its frame.

The wounded man should be easy enough to find later in a camp as small as Hope Creek. Longarm would tend to the other one first.

He moved to the barn, swerving clear of the door, then rammed his left shoulder against it. The smell of musty hay and ammonia wafted from inside. He heard nothing but the creaking timbers, the shifting straw and hay, and the rattle of tack against a ceiling joist.

Quickly, he stepped through the small door and right, pressing his back to the closed double doors, crouching and holding the cocked Colt half out from his side. A mule brayed suddenly, knocking its stall. Longarm jerked with a start, lifting his Colt higher. When the mule settled down, the lawman pricked his ears again, listening for the second bushwhacker.

A gun flashed and roared in the barn's left rear corner. Longarm dropped to both knees as the slug hammered the door behind him. He returned three quick shots at the spot where the flash had been. As the echoes died and the mule commenced braying again in the stygian darkness, boot thuds sounded in the loft, then died suddenly.

When the mule fell silent once more, shuffling around in its stall, a bemused chuckle emanated from the loft.

Longarm moved slowly forward. His eyes had adjusted to the darkness and, with the help of ambient light threading the cracks in the barn walls, he made out the narrow aisle running between the stalls, the ceiling joists from which collars and harnesses hung, and the single, ancient, cavalry-style saddle perched on a saddle partition. The mule continued to nicker and shuffle against its stall as Longarm slowly moved down the aisle, setting each boot down softly.

Dust and straw sifted from the ceiling just ahead and above, and one of the ceiling boards squawked.

Crouching, Longarm emptied his gun into the ceiling—three quick blasts that sounded like dynamite explosions in the close quarters and that set the mule to braying with more raucous fury than before. Boots scuffed in the ceiling, and stopped suddenly.

Longarm stepped back from the place he'd fired from, crouching behind a ceiling joist, and quickly reloaded his Colt. He let the spent casings tumble onto the straw-matted floor with soft snicks that, because of the wind and the indignant mule, wouldn't be heard in the loft.

"How you doin' up there, son of a bitch?" he yelled when the mule had settled down again.

Receiving no response, he moved slowly down the aisle once more, straining his ears to listen, watching for more dust sifting between the ceiling cracks. When he was nearly to the end of the small barn, something ticked against his hat. He lurched back suddenly, crouching and lifting his Colt toward the scarred ceiling planks, but held fire.

Something dribbled down from a knot in one of the planks. Taking his Colt in his gloved hand, he held out his right, felt the warm, oily wetness on his cold fingers.

Blood.

He took his time climbing into the loft. The man was wounded, but Longarm didn't know how bad until he crouched over the figure lying belly down in the hay. The drygulcher was as dead as a beaver hat, shot once in the chest, once in the thigh.

Longarm turned the man over to inspect the fleshy, bearded face. "What's your gripe, you son of a bitch?"

The lawman had a good memory, but he didn't recognize this hombre. If he'd seen his likeness on a wanted dodger, it hadn't been recently, and there was nothing on the man's body, wrapped in a striped coat hand-sewn from trade blankets, that betrayed his identity.

Frustrated, Longarm made his way out of the dark barn and into the starlit night, heading toward the main part of town, the same direction the other bushwhacker had stumbled a few minutes ago. He wanted the second man in good enough condition to answer a few questions.

He'd nearly reached the gap between the two buildings when he stopped. A relatively fresh pile of horse apples lay along the frozen trail. It bore the mark of a boot print.

Longarm continued through the gap cautiously, in the unlikely event the wounded man was still out here and setting another trap. Once through the gap, he angled across the camp's main street toward the saloon from which the guitar and piano music—if you could call it music—seeped from the lighted windows and doors to tear around on the wind. Shadows jostled beyond the windows, men and feather-haired girls tipping their heads back to loose booming laughter at the ceiling.

Longarm planted a boot on the saloon's first wooden step, and stopped. On the second step was a slight smear of green horse dung. On the step above that was a blood smudge.

Longarm's pulse quickened. The second back-shooter had gone into the saloon. Maybe he thought the saloon would be the last place the lawman would look, and if Longarm did come looking for him here, that he could somehow disappear into the crowd.

The lawman pushed through the storm doors and stopped several feet just inside the smoky tavern, his ears reviled by the crowd's booming din and by the piano and the fiddle that had recently replaced the guitar. The piano player was a beefy blond woman in a short, frilly pink dress and with men's long underwear stuffed into miner's boots. She sang while she played, throwing her chin high, but Longarm couldn't make out the words above the din. The man who strummed the fiddle had heavy-lidded eyes and a beard that brushed his sagging paunch.

The heavy warmth, rife with the smell of tobacco smoke, liquor, and sweat, shoved against Longarm like a burial shroud, instantly warming all of his body except his shooting hand, which still felt numb inside his glove and mitten. He looked around the crowded, low-ceilinged room. A couple men glanced back at him, but with only vague interest. They'd likely seen him in here before, drinking and partaking of the free ham and cheese sandwiches.

He moved toward the bar that was two deep with loudly conversing drinkers, most of whose eyes were glassy from several hours of holding the cold at bay. As he passed a table at which four bearded gents were playing poker and speaking German, he nudged a man standing there who was in a red and black mackinaw and had a black wool cap sitting high on his red-haired head.

"You see a man run in here a few minutes ago? Probably walking with a limp?"

The redhead glanced at Longarm, ran his cobalt blue eyes up and down his frame, and frowned with disapproval. "No, I didn't see no one run in here, and what if I did?"

"You might point him out to me," Longarm yelled, competing with the fiddle and the loud Germans.

"The hell I will!" the redhead shouted over the soapy rim of his beer mug.

Longarm brushed past the man. Mining camps were close-knit communities, and people in them tended to mind their own business, expecting the same from others. If a man had run in here, the other drinkers would be damned before they'd point him out to a stranger.

Swinging his head back and forth, looking for a man with a bloody leg, and looking as well for a blood and shit trail on the floor, Longarm shoved his way to the bar, caught the apron's attention, and ordered a rye. Might as well fight the chill from his fingers while he searched for his assailant. When he'd slugged half his drink, he began wandering around the room, shoving and brushing past the miners, store clerks, and painted ladies of Hope Creek, turning down a couple of offers for a tumble in a "right comf'tauble crib out back."

Near the clattering roulette wheel, he stopped and stared at the floor. Near a big Russian miner's hobnailed boot and the green bootie of the girl who stood with her arms around the Russian's neck, lay a green smudge on the scarred puncheons. Another one lay just beyond it, near a table at which one man appeared asleep with his head on his arms and another gent, in a checked shirt and with a green bandanna knotted around his neck, laid out a hand of solitaire.

The sleeping gent—or the one who appeared to be sleeping—sat sideways to Longarm. The other man faced him across the table, a bottle and a glass before him. Longarm could see only the sleeping gent's left leg clad in heavy, much-patched duck trousers. The boot on that foot, however, appeared to have something very closely resembling shit sticking off its sole.

Keeping his eyes on the "sleeping" miner, Longarm pushed through the crowd as he made his way to the table.

Chapter 5

"Out of the way, damnit," Longarm said as he approached the table at which the one man appeared asleep and the other laid out a game of solitaire, moving his lips as though muttering to himself.

"Hey, what's the big idea?" said one of the miners Longarm shoved aside.

"Federal lawman," Longarm said. "Skedaddle."

"Lawman? Well, shit in my *soup*!" the man exclaimed.

At the same time, the man who'd been asleep lifted his head and turned toward Longarm, blinking his brown eyes as though to clear them. He was short and dark, and he wore a cinnamon-colored mustache and goatee, neither of which had been trimmed in a month of Sundays.

Longarm slid his Colt from its holster, and rocked back the hammer. "On your feet, frien—"

Just then the solitaire player leaped out of his chair and, bunching his lips, hefted a long-barreled Colt Army over the table. The gun exploded. The bullet sliced six inches wide of Longarm's head, broke glass behind the bar, and instantly set the crowd to yelling their indignation while those around Longarm ducked or dove for cover.

The shooter, his long, stringy, brown hair flopping around his brutish face, broke and stumbled to Longarm's right, limping heavily on his right leg. When he'd cleared the table, Longarm saw the man's blood-matted thigh. He tried to draw a bead on the scrawny bushwhacker but held fire, as there were too many bystanders around him.

He tracked the man with his Colt, awaiting a clear shot and sidestepping between tables. "You won't make it, friend!"

Just then the bushwhacker, nearly to the stairs rising at the room's rear, grabbed a whore who'd been hiding behind a square-hewn ceiling joist. He pulled the girl in front of him, wrapping one arm around her throat and aiming his long-barreled Colt over her shoulder toward Longarm.

"I'll kill her!" he cried.

The girl, who appeared to have some Indian blood, sunk her teeth into the man's forearm. The man screamed and fired a round into the ceiling.

"You *bitch*!"

The girl tore herself free of the man's grip, cursing in a language Longarm recognized as Ute, and dove for cover beneath a table.

BLAM! BLAM!

Longarm's first shot took the man through his temple, blowing out the opposite side of his head and sending blood, bone, and brains spattering a now-vacant table covered with playing cards and money. Longarm's second shot took the man high in the chest as he swung toward the lawman and began stumbling back toward the stairs.

"Shit!" Longarm barked before the echo of his second shot had died and a half wink before the man overturned two chairs and hit the floor with a thump, gurgling and sputtering as he died.

Longarm had wanted him alive.

Such silence had fallen over the place that Longarm could hear the fires breathing in the two potbelly stoves and the wind howling under the eaves. His boots ground mud and gravel on the floor as he walked over to the dead man lying down with one leg hooked over a fallen chair. The man's eyes were squeezed shut, lips stretched back from his teeth, hands flung out to his sides. His chest was still.

Longarm glanced at the crowd staring at him incredulously, then squatted beside the dead man. He'd just started going through the man's pockets when boots clomped on the porch and the storm doors swung open, squawking amongst the murmurs that had now started to grow in the wake of the shooting.

"What in the hell is goin' on around here?" exclaimed the stocky man in a buffalo robe moving into the room on a chill draft from outside, a scowl bunching his bearded cheeks, a double-barreled shotgun in his hands. "First I hear shootin' over to Vaught's barn, so I go over *there* to investigate. Then I hear shootin' over *here* . . ."

He let his voice trail off as his eyes found Longarm at the back of the room rummaging around in the dead man's pockets.

"You the local law?" Longarm asked, pulling a small scrap of paper from the dead man's shirt pocket. It was a receipt for a paid livery bill, and the name on it was Yancy Carruthers.

The man in the buffalo robe started forward. He wore a long, soiled nightcap, and as he continued toward Longarm, one of the onlookers pulled the cap off his head and tossed it onto a table. Not reacting, the man in the buffalo robe continued forward, scowling at Longarm.

"You the man responsible for all the gunfire around here?" He had a deep, raspy voice. Under his half-buttoned buffalo robe, he wore wash-worn, red long underwear stuffed into stovepipe boots.

"I reckon you could say that," Longarm said, tossing the paper onto the dead man's chest and rising. "I'm Custis Long, deputy United States marshal out of Denver. This gent tried to bushwhack me as I was coming out of the one-holer out back. Same for the dead man you'll find in the loft of the barn you were talkin' about."

The man closed on Longarm, running the back of his hand across his nose and narrowing his eyes suspiciously. "You ain't Custis Long. Longarm? *Bullshit!*"

"I don't recollect havin' had the pleasure, Mister . . . ?"

"Damn, you really are Longarm his ownself? Well, I'll be a monkey's fuckin' uncle!" The man held out his small, freckled hand, a grin now splitting his beard wide open. "Name's Charlie Wainwright. Constable Charlie Wainwright. Pleased to meet you, Marshal. I'm gonna have to go ahead and embarrass myself by telling you honest I'm your biggest fuckin' fan ever. Read about you in the papers all the damn time!"

The murmur of the crowd grew slightly as most of the revelers slipped back into their chairs or turned back to the bar, casting frequent glances at the two lawmen at the back of the room.

"You don't say?" Longarm said. "Well, I tell you, Constable, I'd sure like to know who this fella is and what got him running off his leash at me. Same with the gent in the barn. That receipt there says he's one Yancy Carruthers, but he could have plucked that name out of any ole hat." Longarm turned from the dead man to the still-beaming constable. "You recognize him?"

"Him? Hell, no." Constable Wainwright prodded the dead man with his boot toe. "Just a drifter, I fathom. Seen him and another gent ride in a few days back. If his friend's the stiff in Vaught's barn, I don't know him neither. Never seen either of 'em before in my life. Doubt anyone else around here has, neither. They mostly been keepin' to themselves, playin' poker in here and visiting the cribs out back on occasion."

"They weren't working a claim?"

"If they were, I'd sure like to know how to work one from in here. Hell, I'd give that a shot myself!"

The constable had a good laugh at that. Then Longarm asked him if he'd inquire with the crowd about the dead men's identity. He doubted he'd learn anything, but he had to try. He wanted to know if the dead duo were hired guns or men with personal beefs, if they were working off some long-held grudge or were somehow connected to the job he was currently heading toward—the Tin Cup Trouble.

The constable was pleased to help, but no one

seemed to know anything about the two strangers, including their names, except that one was lousy at poker and the dead man was fair to middling.

"There you have it, Marshal," Wainwright said, throwing out his hands after he'd set two men to the task of hauling the dead men over to the undertaker's. "Maybe those boys recognized you, like I did, and wanted to make names for themselves. Bringin' down a lawman of your reputation would make them pretty tall men in some social circles."

"Maybe," Longarm said, biting off the end of a nickel cheroot and collapsing into the chair the dead man had occupied a few minutes ago.

He had carved a wide swath around the frontier, and made plenty of enemies. But something about these two, Carruthers and his dead friend in the barn, smelled of the Tin Cup Trouble, which was extra troubling. He'd already expected to find about as much trouble as one lawman could handle up thataway, without more spilling down the mountains to greet him.

"Buy ya a drink?" Wainwright said, holding up a bottle and two glasses fresh from the bar.

"Why the hell not?" Longarm said, pensively firing his cheroot.

It was going to be one hell of a long, cold night in Hope Creek.

Longarm and the constable stayed up and chewed the fat for several hours, until they'd drunk themselves nearly oblivious to the weather and the wailing of the portly, piano-hammering, pink-clad blonde, and Wainwright ambled off mumbling something about wishing he had a warm whore waiting for him under the blankets instead of a chill Presbyterian wife.

Longarm moseyed upstairs to his rented digs above the saloon, where he shared the tight, drafty quarters with two loudly snoring miners. Across the room, some gent called Quirt was throwing the bedsprings to a whore who had an annoyingly girlish voice and who kept saying over and over, amidst Quirt's grunts and sighs, "Damn, I'm just chilled to the *bone!*"

In spite of the noise and a pillow that smelled as though it had been smuggled out of a bear den, Longarm slept well enough, using his own bedroll in addition to the two wool army blankets supplied by the saloon. In the morning, he ate a quick breakfast downstairs before the train whistle blew on the hill west of the town.

Gathering his bedroll and his rifle, he bid adieu to Hope Creek—which looked and felt more like Hopeless Creek even in daylight, under a cloudy sky, a stiff wind creaking the cabins and swirling the smoke from the breakfast fires and the snow dusting the iron-hard wheel ruts.

He and the other passengers, who numbered around twelve, most of whom had slept in a boardinghouse on the east side of town, trudged through the tall pines and firs, the women wrapped in quilts and blankets, the men leaning into the wind and holding their hats on their heads. It was a two-hundred-yard hike across a steep mountain shoulder to the train, rumbling on the narrow-gauge tracks under a heavy cloud of black smoke wafting from the locomotive's diamond-shaped stack.

The snow piled on either side of the tracks and under

the pines was dishwater gray and laden with pine nee-
dles and squirrel shit.

Longarm helped an old woman through the drift,
holding a burlap-wrapped cage of newly hatched, peep-
ing chicks. How the woman had kept the little birds
alive in this temperature, he couldn't fathom. He didn't
try to ask her because she didn't speak a lick of anything
but Norwegian or Swedish or one of those other cold
northern European tongues. She didn't seem to mind the
weather; she did nothing but laugh gaily while he helped
her through the snow and hefted her considerable bulk
onto the train's single passenger car, then handed up the
chicks.

The train traced a long, slow, winding course through
the mountains, the northern slopes of which were still
buried under several feet of dirty snow. Hopeful signs
that spring was near were a young moose calf and its
mother sunning themselves on a sunny hillside under a
clear blue sky, with snowmelt broiling down the willow-
sheathed ravine beside them and dozens of bluebirds
flitting about flooded beaver meadows.

The train arrived in the little valley town of Gunnison
two days after leaving Hope Creek. Longarm rented a
horse at the town's only livery and feed stable—a
hearty-looking buckskin named Duke—and after getting
directions from the liveryman, started on his horseback
trek northeast along the Taylor River. The ride took him
another two days and two bone-splintering nights
camped beside the river that churned and broiled in a
frothy, spring fervor down the steep-walled, fir-choked
canyon.

Following the liveryman's directions, at the top of

the Taylor watershed he swerved east from the river, past a small ranch outfit nestled in the sage at the mouth of a wide valley rimmed in peaks as white as wedding cakes. The altitude here made his ears ring and his heart beat faster. He followed a wagon trail through the middle of the valley until pines spilled down from the ridges on both sides and a humble wooden sign appeared along the trail, in the shade of one such pine, announcing TIN CUP, COLO. TERR. Beneath the board sign was a slightly larger one, warning in red letters: CLAIM JUMPERS BE-WARE! It wasn't until a few minutes later that the trees fell back behind Longarm and he topped a broad flat bowl in the mountains filled with cabins, tents, tipples, Long Toms, barking dogs, and the smells of raw sewage and moldering trash that were part and parcel of any mining camp.

"I'd be obliged if you'd direct me to the town marshal's office," Longarm said with a pinch of his hat brim to a beefy gent with long shaggy hair falling from the sides of his otherwise bald head. He was hammering an iron rim on a wagon wheel between the open double doors of a log-and-canvas blacksmith shop.

The man merely looked up from his work to point his hammer down the narrow street to Longarm's left, his blue eyes unfriendly, and then continued shaping the rim with the hammer.

"Thanks, friend," Longarm grumbled, heeling Duke down the side street, noting shingles for a gentleman's apparel store, a harness shop, a café calling itself simply Good Food, and a Charles C. Johns Drug Emporium, though the size of the place—merely a peak-roofed log cabin little larger than a Conestoga argonaut wagon,

with blue smoke skeining from its tin chimney pipe—
belied the moniker.

Longarm was three quarters down the street, the end
of which rose into piney, boulder-studded hills, when he
started angling toward a log hovel about the same size
as the drug emporium and with a shingle announcing
MARSHAL. A gun popped behind him. A man shouted.
Duke gave an indignant whinny and bucked, all four
hooves leaving the ground as he twisted and turned his
bulky body.

Before Longarm was able to process the gunshot as
well as the horse's sudden, violent reaction to it, he
found himself hurling through midair. His stomach rose
into his throat as he watched in the periphery of his vision the ground fly up beneath him to smack him without ceremony on his back and shoulders, the breath
leaving his lungs in one violent *whufff!*

Chapter 6

The gun popped again. Longarm winced and lifted his cheek from the cold mud that was a foot deep in the narrow trace.

Here we go again.

As the buckskin galloped down the street, trailing its reins and loosing shrill, indignant whinnies, Longarm rose to his knees and snaked his gloved right hand across his belly for his .44. A man ran across the street behind him. Another one ran up the street toward Longarm, stopping between the drug emporium and the gentleman's apparel—a short man in a shabby suitcoat over a red plaid shirt and with shaggy blond hair poking out around a ratty bowler hat. He stopped and aimed at the man who'd run across the street.

"Stop or take it in the back, Lionel, you thievin' *dawg*!"

The gun popped and smoked. The bullet plunked into a tent stake on the other side of the street. The man the bowler-hatted gent had fired on, a big man with a buckskin shirt and long, black hair falling from a funnel-brimmed hat, stopped and wheeled, bringing up an old Colt Navy.

"Don't you *dare* shoot at me, you son of a bitch!" warned the bowler-hatted gent, extending an admonishing finger.

The big man's Colt smoked and popped. The bowler-hatted gent lifted his right foot suddenly, screaming and prancing before tumbling into the sage and mud and firing a wild shot at the big man, who wheeled and continued past the tent and out of sight.

"Laramie, doggone it!" another man shouted, running up from the direction of the marshal's office. He wore a silver star on his brown vest and carried a long-barreled, double-bore Greener up high across his chest. "What'd I tell you about discharging your firearm in the city limits?"

As he crossed a wide gap between cabins, he glanced at Longarm. "Holster your hogleg, mister. This ain't about you!"

Then he continued to the bowler-hatted gent, who was rolling around on his butt and clutching his right foot with both hands, cursing.

Wincing at the pain shooting through both shoulders and one hip, Longarm depressed his Colt's trigger and climbed to his feet. He glanced around to see his buckskin standing outside a tent shack, its reins held by a short, squat, dark-skinned man in a low-crowned black hat and a billowing apron who was staring toward Longarm. Longarm waved at the man holding his horse, then, brushing mud off his cheek and his black frock coat, moved stiffly toward the marshal. The local lawman was down on one knee beside the cursing, writhing man called Laramie.

"It don't look that bad, you fool. He just creased your boot toe's all."

"Hurts like hell!" Laramie screamed. "I think that dirty dog mighta blowed my little toe off!"

"It'd suit you right if he had!" The marshal grabbed the man's pistol from the mud and rose, continuing to stare down at the writhing Laramie. "I'm gonna confiscate this till you're ready to head back to your diggin's, and if you ever . . . *ever!* . . . discharge a firearm in town again, you'll never set foot in Tin Cup again in your life. You'll have to haul your dust and oil your tonsils all the way over the pass to Buena Vista!"

The marshal delivered a vicious kick to Laramie's backside. "Now, git up and *vamoose!*"

Laramie made a great to-do, sobbing and groaning about heaving himself to his feet. When he'd finally made it, giving the marshal an indignant look, and commenced hopping off between the cabins toward the other side of the camp while having to fend off a dog that ran out from beneath a cabin porch to bark and nip at his heels, the marshal turned toward Longarm standing beside him.

"Sorry about that, mister," the local lawman said, wiping mud from the barrel of Laramie's old hogleg. He was a few inches shorter than Longarm—a good-looking gent, clean-shaven, roughly Longarm's age and wearing a black derby, with armbands on the sleeves of his pinstriped shirt. "Hope you didn't get hurt none."

"Just my pride," Longarm said. "What's ole Laramie's beef with the big man?"

"Claims he's been jumpin' Laramie's claims . . . again. Happens about two or three times a spring.

Shame of it all is ole Lionel is Laramie's brother-in-
law." The marshal inspected Longarm's muddy coat and
whipcord trousers. "Like I said, you have my apologies.
Looks like Milton's bringin' your horse back. Well, if
you'll excuse me . . ."

He brushed a hand across his dimpled chin and
started for the jailhouse.

"Hold on, Marshal. I'm the federal you sent for. Custis Long out of Denver." Longarm showed the man his
badge in the palm of his gloved hand. He rarely wore
the badge unless he was making an arrest or wandering
the halls of the Denver Federal Building. Nothing attracted trouble better than a federal copper badge.

"Oh, thank Christ!" the local lawman said, dropping
his chin and shoulders with a visible show of relief. "I
didn't think you'd ever get here. Please, come. Follow
me back to my office for a cup of coffee, and I'll fill
you in."

"My boss, Chief Marshal Billy Vail, roughed out
the general picture," Longarm said as they slopped
through the mud left by snowdrifts still melting in the
shade of the cabins. "But I reckon I'm gonna need a
few details—such as directions to this woman's cabin—
the one whose husband robbed the stage and started the
ball rollin'."

"Yes, of course," the marshal said. "I'll give you
everything you need. I'm just so happy to have a little
help—*federal* help! You don't know what it's been
like . . ."

The man let the sentence trail off as, passing a cabin
from which three scantily clad Chinese girls peered out
from an open door, whispering and giggling as they

sized up the big stranger in the snuff brown hat, the local lawman stopped suddenly before the cabin's stock trough. He chuffed ironically, removed his glove from his right hand, and extended the hand to Longarm. "I'm sorry. Listen to me go on without even introducing myself. I'm Chester Dobie, deputy marshal of Tin Cup. Although now I guess you could say I'm acting marshal, since Marshal Lewis was back-shot nigh on a month ago now, and I was his only deputy."

Longarm shook the man's hand. "I understand your predicament. One man against a town full of raving lunatics is what the report makes it sound like."

"It's a whole lot worse than that." Dobie started for his office once more, but stopped again abruptly and turned to the muttering, giggling Chinese girls. "Oh, those there are Marmalade, Punkin' Boots, and Columbine. They run a bath and laundry house and"—the marshal winked at Longarm—"a whole lot more, if you get my drift. Girls, this here's Deputy U.S. Marshal Custis Long out of Denver. He's come to give me a hand."

Longarm pinched his hat brim and winked at the three pretty, round-faced girls, all wearing silk kimonos of different colors and designs.

"Now that your curiosity's been satisfied, you can run along," the marshal told the girls, all three still eyeing Longarm admiringly, one raising her hand as if to indicate "tall."

Dobie and Longarm continued toward the marshal's office.

"As you can see," the marshal said, throwing out an arm to indicate the shacks around him, "those three and damn few others are the only ones left in the town. Everyone else is out lookin' for that loot they think's buried out in the mountains."

"Isn't there enough gold to keep people to home working?"

"Not at the moment. Two summers ago was our biggest year. Nearly two million dollars in high-grade ore was carved out of these mountains or washed out of the streams. Since then, the miners have been making just enough to keep them here breaking rocks. Can't even afford to pull up stakes and move on. We have a stamping mill on the other side of the town, at the big Kokomo digging, but it's silent all but two, three times a week these days. Not enough ore to make it worth starting up and shutting down. Takes man power and steam power, don't ya know."

As they mounted the boardwalk fronting the little log jailhouse, Longarm yelled his appreciation toward the back of the dark man who'd tied his buckskin to the hitch rack fronting the marshal's office. The man merely threw an arm out in acknowledgment.

"That's Pedro Estevan," Dobie said. "Brews ale and does odd jobs around the camp." Dobie glanced over his shoulder at Longarm, then canted his head. "Come here—let me show you something."

Dobie strode past the jailhouse's open front door and stopped at the building's opposite front corner. He threw an arm out to indicate the rear of a barnlike log structure behind the jailhouse and to the left of it, about fifty yards away, on a separate lot that faced the opposite direction. There, a man was planing the side of one of the three pine coffins he had propped on sawhorses.

Two more coffins, standing upright, leaned against

the barn wall flanking the man. Each coffin contained what from even this distance Longarm recognized as dead men, their hair perfectly combed, collars buttoned, stiff arms crossed on their chests. Both cadavers, men in their twenties, wore sapsucker smiles, as though they knew some secret the man planing the coffin did not.

"That there is Everett Turnbull, the local undertaker," Dobie said as the man continued planing, oblivious of the marshal's and Longarm's scrutiny. "And them two in the wooden overcoats are the Hill brothers, shot dead in the mountains south of here while they were looking for the stolen stage loot. A boy out hunting jackrabbits found 'em in a ravine near the old mine shack cellar they'd been digging in, hoping to find the loot."

"Who're the other three coffins for?"

"The next three killed in the trouble."

Longarm cocked an eyebrow at the town marshal.

"Turnbull is a businessman, and he believes in being prepared," the marshal said grimly. "Tin Cup might be on the bust side of its boom, but since that stage robbery last summer, with everyone and their mother scouring the draws and creek bottoms for it, Turnbull's been goin' to bed every night with a big, shit-eating grin on his face. He's grinning right now, Marshal Long. You maybe can't see it because of his hat brim, but take my word for it—Everett Turnbull's a happy man."

The Tin Cup marshal brushed past Longarm and stepped into the jailhouse. "Come on inside and have a cup of java. I'll answer your questions and give you directions to the Duchaine place. I sure as shit hope you can convince that conniving woman to tell you where the loot's buried, but I hold little hope. Dalia Duchaine is as stubborn as she is pretty."

Longarm removed his hat and, flicking more mud from his shoulder, ducked through the door. The marshal's office wasn't much—a desk, a few shelves, a gun rack that held two Spencer repeaters with a chain through their trigger guards. In the middle of the shadowy, wood-floored room, a potbelly stove ticked, and a dented black percolator chugged softly on the stove's warming plate. There was a stout wooden door with a single barred window at the back; it likely led to the cell block.

Marshal Dobie leaned his shotgun against the wall, poured himself and Longarm each a black tin cup of smoking coffee, then slumped into his spool-back chair, doffing his hat and wearily running his hands through his thick, wavy hair. "Have a seat." He opened his hand toward the chair fronting his desk—another hide-bottom spool-back that looked so flimsy, Longarm wasn't sure it would hold his 190 pounds without crumbling into matchsticks.

It creaked beneath his muscular bulk and, holding his breath, he leaned slightly forward, setting his hat on his thighs. He didn't dare lean back, as the chair back would surely send him sprawling.

"Oh, go ahead," Dobie said, kicking back in his own chair and crossing his boots on his desktop. "I reinforced that chair and this one myself. Got tired of falling over backward and rolling around on the floor like a damn moron. I'm a furniture maker by trade."

Longarm leaned slowly back in the chair, testing its strength. It creaked but seemed solid. "Damn, you rein-

forced her good. Doesn't look like it'd hold a pissant."
He relaxed, hiked a boot on his knee, and plucked a cheroot from his shirt pocket, firing a lucifer on his heel.
"First off," he said, blowing smoke and waving out the
match, "call me Longarm. All my friends and enemies
do."

"Heard of you," Dobie said. "I was hoping they'd
send you."

"Gotta question for you. You don't happen to know a
gent called Yancy Carruthers, do you?"

Dobie frowned as he absently turned his coffee cup
on his desk. "Should I?"

"No should about it. A man going by that handle
tried to bushwhack me outside a one-hole privy in Hope
Creek a couple days ago on my way up here. Him and
another fella, both of 'em now doin' the two-step with
El Diablo."

Longarm sipped his coffee and set the cup on his
knee, holding it there with one hand while he held the
cheroot with the other. "Now, I've plenty of folks want-
ing to ventilate my hide, but I didn't recognize either
one of those privy rats. They could be guns hired by
someone I pissed off on another job—their brother dead
or in prison on account of me or some such. On the
other hand, they might've come from here. And if I've
already made enemies here—which is fast even for
me—I'd like to know who they are."

"In other words, who other than me knows I sent for
you?" Dobie sipped his coffee, frowning toward the
open door through which the high-mountain sunlight
angled. "Hell, I might've made mention to any number
of folks. I don't have too many friends around here, but

there's a few I confide in, and I didn't see any reason *not* to tell 'em I'd sent for federal assistance."

"Me neither," Longarm said. "I was just curious about the two bushwhackers, that's all. Now that that's unresolved, tell me about the Widow Duchaine's dearly departed husband—this Tin Cup Pete. Knowing something about him might help me track the loot he supposedly buried . . . if the widow doesn't have it, that is."

Dobie hiked a shoulder. "Pete was an odd one. He got the name Tin Cup because, when he first got here—and he was one of the *first* here—he was so poor that he panned for an entire month with a tin cup. Little by little, he found color, but it never really amounted to much. He loved the country, though, so he stayed here, built a ranch just over the divide to the west, and married the daughter of a freighter—the former Miss Dalia Hagen. Don't ask me what the attraction was for her. Pete was tall and nearly bald—an ugly cuss with a big, broken nose. As for Dalia . . ."

The marshal rose, retrieved the coffeepot from the potbelly stove, and gave Longarm a warm-up before rewarming his own. "Dalia's a piece of work. A brown-eyed blonde. Mid-twenties. Damn sportin' figure. Pete fell head over heels, totally devoted to the woman. I don't know if Dalia put Pete up to robbing that stage or not—I don't know her well enough, though I do know she was raised a staunch German Catholic—but that's the word goin' around. She's a right feisty, fiery girl, and if she knows where the money is—and who else *would* know, since Pete robbed the stage for her after all!—good luck trying to get it out of her."

"If she had it," Longarm said, turning his head to

watch through the building's single window as a couple of mongrel dogs trotted down the nearly deserted main street, tongues drooping, "wouldn't she have skipped the country with it by now? Didn't you say her husband robbed the stage last summer?"

Dobie nodded as he swallowed the strong, hot brew. "I s'pose that was the plan. Maybe she—and ole Pete—didn't figure on this much of a to-do about the money. If she skipped now with the strongbox, she'd be run down in days."

"So you figure she's waiting for everybody to settle down, maybe forget the whole thing, and *then* move on."

"That's what I'd do."

"Sounds right enough. One more question before I light out for the Duchaine place." Longarm sipped the brew and chewed his cigar thoughtfully. "Where was the marshal shot and what kind of a trail was he sniffing?"

"Up near Mirror Lake. Someone—I don't know who—said they'd seen Tin Cup Pete up around there the day before he turned himself in for the holdup. His conscience got the better of him. He walked in here unarmed and with his hands up, chin dipped to his chest. Anyway, Marshal Lewis was found on the shore of the lake in a pool of his own blood—back-shot."

"You don't say." Longarm blew smoke at the rafters, his mind riffling through all the small details, sorting them, trying to figure it all out. After he'd climbed out of his chair and stood in the open doorway, looking over the buckskin and into the muddy, sun-washed street, he said, "Regarding Mirror Lake, did you check it out?"

"Yep. A hell of a lot of snow up there a couple weeks ago. Probably still some. When the drifts recede, I'll go have another look. It seems unlikely to me, though, that Pete would travel all the way to the other side of Tin Cup from his ranch to hide the loot. Hell, there are plenty of places around his own ranch without traveling nearly twenty miles." Dobie shook his head and lifted his cup to his lips, draining it.

"Well, that oughta do it," Longarm said. "If you'll draw me a map of the area, marking all the hot spots, I'll start fogging the pines."

Dobie plucked a lined notepad from a drawer and plopped it onto his desk. "Sure you don't want to call it a day, start fresh in the morning? If you leave now, you're liable to get caught out after dark. And these mountains get *dark*!"

"I been cooling my heels for four days on the train ride up here. I'm ready to start turning over some rocks."

"Be careful," Dobie said when he'd sketched out a detailed map in pencil and handed it across the desk to Longarm. "There's bears fresh out of hibernation in them mountains and canyons—the human kind as well as the furry kind, and these days I don't know which ones are worse."

Chapter 7

The Duchaine spread sat in a sun-splashed mountain meadow, a grassy pasture and a chuckling creek behind it. Behind the pasture and the creek rose a pine-covered ridge. The trail Longarm had taken out from Tin Cup, traversing three divides and splashing through twice that many creeks and spring freshets, meandered in front of it, running along the pine-clad ridge to the north.

Sitting a rocky knoll just east of the place, Longarm scrutinized the headquarters through his field glasses. It wasn't much—just a two-story, chinked-log cabin with a wide stone hearth abutting the side nearest Longarm, with a privy and a kitchen garden out back. There were two or three corrals, a small barn, a springhouse, and a dilapidated wagon on the shady western side of the springhouse. A nicely figured blond woman—likely Mrs. Duchaine herself—was mucking manure from the barn, tossing the soiled hay out the open doors with a pitchfork. A Winchester carbine leaned against the barn wall, within easy reach of the doors.

Longarm remembered what the marshal had said

about the woman being feisty. He also remembered that she'd also shot a man trespassing on her property.

Deciding it might be prudent to ride in from the rear of the headquarters, where the trees would cover him until he got into the yard and could show the woman his badge before she tried a long-distance shot with her carbine, he slipped the field glasses back into the war bag draped over his saddle horn. He clucked the buckskin down off the knoll and into a flooded beaver meadow, splashing through the forking, willow-sheathed stream toward the southern ridge.

When he made the pines along the ridge, he headed west toward the ranch headquarters, staying in the tall pines through which the angling sun washed like liquid gold, and the tang of pine sap and spring humus was heavy in his nostrils. Hummingbirds buzzed about the blooming red columbine, woodpeckers hammered the tree trunks, and angry squirrels chittered, scurrying about the branches overhanging Longarm and occasionally loosing a pine cone onto the trail and making the rather jumpy buckskin flinch and nicker.

"Easy does it, Duke," Longarm growled, noting the ache that had remained in his shoulder after his unceremonious, not to mention embarrassing, unseating earlier in Tin Cup. "The liveryman didn't tell me you were so damn owly. He was probably playing a joke on the federal outta Denver. Prob'ly having himself a good laugh over an ale with his pards even as we ride . . ."

When Longarm saw the corrals at the rear of the ranch headquarters through the trees, he swung Duke straight north, then drew back on his reins suddenly. "Whoa!"

Between two arrow-straight firs lay a hole roughly four by four feet square, with several pine boughs angled into it from the sides. Longarm scrutinized the hole curiously. It didn't look natural, but there was no dirt pile nearby. Finally, he swung down from the leather and, holding the buckskin's reins in one hand, strode over to the side of the hole and peered inside.

He jerked back slightly with a start as he saw two glaring brown eyes staring back up at him from the bottom of the pit. A wince followed when he saw that the two eyes belonged to a man—a mustached gent with long, dark brown hair and wearing a green wool mackinaw, a red scarf knotted around his neck. He was slumped backward from his waist, arms drooping down around the sharpened aspen branches jutting up from the bottom of the hole and impaling him throughout his chest and crotch, with another poking up out of his thigh.

The sharpened tips of the bayonetlike branches were brown with dried blood.

The man stared up in hushed awe at Longarm, lower jaw hanging, mouth forming a near-perfect O, teeth hidden by his lips. His tongue shone dimly, curled back inside his mouth.

"Bear trap."

Longarm hunkered on a knee beside the hole, grabbing one of the fir boughs the pit had obviously been covered with before the man had stepped backward into it, maybe having heard a sound from his backtrail. The man was still in good shape, as far as cadavers went. He'd probably taken his misstep as recently as last night or even early this morning. Down near his mule-eared moccasin boots lay a Springfield rifle.

Longarm sighed and shook his head. "Bad way to go, friend. But look at it this way. You probably just barely knew what hit you before St. Pete was shakin' your hand. We should all be so lucky."

Looking around carefully for more bear traps or any other kind of a trap, Longarm stepped into his saddle and urged Duke around the gaping pit toward the rear of the ranch headquarters. He felt a prickling beneath his collar and, automatically, he reached forward and pulled his Winchester '73 from the sheath under his right thigh. He cocked it quietly and, planting the butt snug against his cartridge belt, walked the horse slowly forward, keeping his eyes and ears alert to the small outbuildings and corrals growing before him.

There was a smaller cabin back here, with a connecting corral, both grown up with weeds, the cabin's tin chimney pipe badly rusted. It was probably the place's original hut, abandoned when Tin Cup Pete built the sturdier, larger cabin closer to the trail. As Longarm swung right of the corral, hurried footsteps sounded on the cabin's other side. The lawman clucked to the horse, and they trotted forward. When he was behind the cabin's east wall, Longarm slid down from Duke's back, slid his Winchester into its saddle boot, dropped the buckskin's reins, and palmed his .44.

"Stay, boy," he whispered, striding up the side of the cabin.

He sneaked a peek around the front, then hurried through the sagebrush and bluestem to the opposite corner. A rifle cracked—once, twice, three times.

He doffed his hat, looked around the corner. At the cabin's rear, the woman stood holding the Winchester carbine over a corral slat, sliding the barrel this way and that as she peered across the meadow toward the piney ridge from which Longarm had come.

"I know you're out there!" she shouted, racking another shell into the carbine's breech.

She fired two more shots into the meadow, blowing up dust and sage branches. Longarm hurried up behind her, her shots covering his footsteps. As she ejected a spent cartridge and racked another, Longarm reached around in front of her, grabbed the Winchester with one hand, and pulled up and back.

She hadn't been ready for him, but she held on to the gun anyway, giving a ferocious grunt. She'd have been better off releasing the carbine, because Longarm was stronger than she was, and his violent wrenching of the gun from her grasp spun her around. Losing her footing, she fell sideways into the sage at the base of the cabin, crying, "Son of a *bitch*!"

Lying on her shoulder and hip, she looked up at him, jaws hard and brown eyes blazing red-gold fire. Longarm stepped back, raising the Winchester's barrel and quickly ejecting three live rounds into the breeze-brushed grass. Setting the rifle over his shoulder and holding the woman's wildcat gaze with his own, he felt a rippling down the muscles in his back. Dobie had warned him she was pretty, but he hadn't been prepared for this blond-haired, brown-eyed beauty glaring up at him like a hungry cat staring at prey.

The skin of her face was smooth and tan, the Germanic cheekbones high and wide. Her eyes were saddle-leather brown, shiny as polished marbles. They were almond-shaped, with tiny lines spoking from their corners, and he didn't know if the lines were due to her rage or if they were always like that, but they added to her fierce, alluring power as well as told him this was no schoolgirl he was dealing with, but a full-grown woman practically Longarm's own age.

The first three buttons of her simple white blouse were undone, allowing a heart-twisting view of her ample cleavage and the ripe orbs housed below that, with the sharp rising and falling of each angry breath, threatened to break free of their insubstantial cotton harness. Her rich, gold-blond hair had been secured in a French braid, but the braid had come loose in the fall, and the thick golden swirls falling down the back of her tan neck like clover honey added to her appearance of primal, female power.

Through gritted teeth, she spat, "You're trespassing on private property, you son of a bitch, and I'll see you hanged!"

"Since when's trespassing become a hanging offense?"

"Since you trespassed on *my* property!"

"Well, that's gonna be kinda hard for you to do, unless you've got someone else around here. When I glassed the place a half hour ago, you were the only one I saw." Longarm shook his head with appreciation, unable to keep his eyes from leaping left and right across her sprawled, sexy frame. "And I gotta tell you, Mrs. Duchaine, you were enough."

Remaining on one elbow, her tan cheeks dark with rage, eyes narrowed to slits, she shouted, "Go fuck yourself, since it's likely no one else would want to, and *give me my Winchester back*!"

Longarm tossed her carbine into the grass butt down,

the barrel falling over her body to lean barrel up against the cabin wall. Before she could grab it, he thumbed his badge from the lower pocket of his vest and chucked it into the grass about one inch in front of her heaving bosom.

She cut short her reach for the rifle, and looked down at the badge. Frowning, she picked it up in one hand and held it in front of her face. Still frowning, she lifted her gaze above the badge to Longarm standing six feet away from her, feet spread, thumbs hooked behind his cartridge belt, a wry grin on his lips mantled by a thick, longhorn mustache.

Somehow her barn talk, unexpected from one so classically beautiful, added to her allure, and he suppressed the hammering of his heart against his rib cage.

"U.S. marshal?" she said.

"Deputy."

Mrs. Duchaine winced as she pushed up off her elbow. Holding her right wrist in the other hand, which was still holding his badge, she sat up against the cabin wall, laying the empty Winchester in the grass and bending her legs to one side beneath her long, spruce green skirt held tight to her narrow waist by a wide, gold-buckled black belt.

"What the hell do you want with me? And just because you're federal doesn't mean you can trespass on *private* property. I know a little something about the Constitution of the United States."

"I bet you do." She was indeed no superficial-looking beauty. Her eyes owned a keen, wry intelligence. "I'm here to check into the trouble you seem to be at the center of. What's wrong with your wrist?"

"It hurts," she said through gritted teeth, opening and closing her hand. "No thanks to you jerking that rifle out of my hands when I have every right to protect myself."

"Well, you see, you have a reputation for shooting first and asking questions later. Though the gent I saw in your bear trap yonder didn't even have that kindness bestowed upon him before he sort of prematurely expired." Longarm hunkered down before her, and reached for her hand. "Let me see."

"Leave me alone!" She pulled her hand back, flaring her eyes at him once again. Then, more softly, and with the edge burning out of her gaze, "Dobie called you in?"

"That's right."

"And I suppose you're here to torture the whereabouts of the strongbox from me."

"Something like that."

Mrs. Duchaine glanced at the cartridges in the grass and sage before her. "Well, looks like there's no getting shed of you till you've asked your questions." She pushed to her feet with one hand, pressing her injured wrist against her stomach. "Might as well come in for some coffee."

"I'd be obliged." Longarm stooped to pick up the .44 shells and the woman's rifle.

"Don't go getting polite on me or I won't know what to make of you," the woman said, walking up the side of the cabin, still holding her wrist to her belly.

Holding the woman's rifle over his shoulder, the cartridges in the palm of his other hand, Longarm strode along beside her. "Just doing my job, Mrs. Duchaine."

"Since we're getting so friendly, I suppose you might as well call me Dalia. Everyone else does . . . those I let on the place anyway, and since you're here and there's nothing I can do about it."

"What about the gent in the bear trap?"

"I honestly didn't know anyone was out there. I guess that explains the saddle horn that was foraging around my kitchen garden this morning." As they passed the privy and headed for the rear of the main cabin, Dalia Duchaine glanced at Longarm, frowning. "He's dead, I take it?"

"Since last night most likely. It's a right effective pit."

"Pete dug it two years ago, when a rogue grizzly was preying on our stock. When we still *had* some stock, that is, before the last couple of brutal winters. I'll admit I covered that hole with pine boughs after this trouble started, because I got sick and tired of men coming onto the place who had no business here except to try to cajole and threaten me into telling them where my husband hid the stagecoach money."

She glanced at Longarm again as she opened the cabin's back door, the wind wisping her honey gold hair about her determined, brown eyes. "And I have every right to protect myself."

"Yes, ma'am, you do. Especially a woman out here alone." Longarm looked down at her wryly as he reached over her head to hold the door open. "But you might want to check your traps on occasion and, just for the sake of decorum if nothing else, report your dead to the marshal in Tin Cup, since he seems to have jurisdiction over this part of the county."

She curled her nose at him and ducked under his arm as she turned into the cabin.

"I'll be along in a minute," Longarm told her, hand-ing her the rifle and the live cartridges. "I'm gonna check on my horse. He's the skittish type, and after all your shooting, I might be walking back to Tin Cup."

With that, he closed the door. A minute later, walk-ing around to the front of the cabin, he found Duke standing by the corral by the barn, hanging his head over the top unskinned pine pole as if to say howdy-do to the four horses facing him, all standing stock-still except for swishing their tails sociably. Three were likely the woman's—two good quarter horses and an Appaloosa, all obviously well cared for. Longarm would have bet dollars to doughnuts the fourth horse—a hammer-headed line-back dun—belonged to the man in the bear trap.

He walked over, unsaddled Duke, and turned him into the corral, where the horse snorted a friendly greet-ing to the others, then promptly rolled in the dust. The others watched the buckskin obliquely, the Appaloosa shaking its head and lifting a frisky whinny.

Leaving his gear draped over the top corral slat, Long-arm tramped back to the cabin, crossed the stout front porch, and pushed the front door open. "Mrs. Duchaine?" he called into the shadowy house.

"I'm in the kitchen."

"Just making sure you hadn't loaded that Winches-ter."

"I have," she said dryly above the sqawking of a wa-ter pump. "But it's on the table."

Longarm crossed the well-appointed front room, half of which served as a parlor with a couple of rocking chairs, a small leather couch, and a thick, braided rug sprawled before the hearth in which a small fire popped and snapped. The back half of the room was obviously the dining area, occupied as it was by a sideboard, a hanging, glass-doored cabinet, and a large dining table adorned with only a single gas lamp resting atop a white doily.

Longarm stopped in the doorway to the kitchen. He was glad to see the Winchester on the rough-hewn table along the back wall. It had occurred to him just after he'd returned the rifle and shells to her that she could drygulch him easily enough when he returned to the house. Longarm wasn't normally the trusting type, but he found himself instinctively trusting this woman. He wasn't sure if that trust was due to anything more than her well-filled blouse and shimmering stare, but there it was.

His lust might get him killed before the day was over, but she seemed as straightforward as a plains mule train, though a whole lot prettier.

She was working the pump handle over the wooden sink with her left hand, holding her injured right one down by her side and bunching her lips with the effort. He admired the way each lunge made her ripe breasts jostle inside her blouse, but he went over and nudged her aside. "Here—I'll do that."

"Damn wrist," she said, setting out a tin of Arbuckle's. "It doesn't hurt unless I use it."

"So don't use it. Sit down. I'll make the coffee."

"I reckon it's the least you could do," she said ironically, dragging a chair out from the rough-hewn food-preparation table, smoothing her skirt against her bottom, and sitting down.

He kept her and the loaded rifle in the periphery of

his vision as he filled a percolator and dumped in a couple of handfuls of the store-ground coffee. The iron range was hot, but he lifted a burner lid, dropped another chunk of pine through the hole to stoke it, then plopped the lid back into place with a clank and set the percolator on top of it.

The pot instantly began singing as it heated.

"By the way you make coffee, you must be a bachelor," she said, her ironic smile in place, one leg crossed over the other, her injured hand in her lap.

Longarm doffed his hat, and tossed it on the table. "Tracking outlaws is dangerous enough without having a woman to spar with at home."

"I have a feeling you could hold your own with the fairer sex, Marshal Long. You certainly had me dead to rights."

"Only because I spied your bear bait yonder and got the drop." He dragged a chair out and sat down. "Call me Longarm. Everyone else does."

She arched a brow the same honey shade as her hair. "Long arm of the law?"

"More or less." He reached into his shirt pocket and held up a nickel cheroot. "Mind if I smoke?"

"Long as you don't mind me not joining you."

When he fired the cheroot and blew smoke toward a window, he waved out the match and tossed it onto a tin plate littered with toast crumbs. He flicked a fleck of tobacco from his mustache and leveled a stare at the ironically smiling woman seated at the end of the table, facing him with unconcealed interest.

"Now, then, where do you s'pose that strongbox is, Dalia?"

"Even before we've had our coffee?" She gave an expression of mock surprise. "You'd better slow down, Marshal. We've got a long night ahead."

"Who says I'm stayin'?"

"I do."

Chapter 8

Longarm slid both flaps of the cotton blouse away from the high, proud breasts and cupped them over the even lighter, lacy fabric of the chemise, squeezing and lifting until both swollen, pear-shaped orbs sprang free of the garment and fell down over the top, fully exposed.

One strap of the chemise tumbled down Dalia Duchaine's thin, muscular arm beneath the blouse, and she groaned and swooned as Longarm, lifting his head from the pillow, closed his mouth over each nipple in turn, caressing it with his tongue and sucking. Ripples of ecstasy shuddered through her as he suckled and caressed her breasts with his lips and his mustache, the mushroom head of his piston-hard shaft jutting up between her thighs and edging inside the yielding portals of her warm moistness.

"Ohhhhh," she whispered, throwing her head back on her shoulders. "Ohhhh . . ."

Finally, holding her on top of him with one arm, he rose to a sitting position, pulling her legs around his waist. Placing his hands on her thighs, he slid her hips

toward him, and she gave another throaty groan as his
cock slid slowly inside her until his balls pricked with
the hair of her warm, wet snatch.

They rocked together for a time, Dalia Duchaine's
legs entwined around his waist, her arms around his
back as she nuzzled his neck, kissing him gently and
groaning and sighing in his ear. Longarm splayed his
fingers across her full buttocks, pulling her taut against
him, then using the heels of his hands against her hips to
push her away before pulling her forward once more, his
shaft sliding deep, deep, and her breasts mashing nearly
flat against his chest.

It was a rapturous coupling, the rutting of two adults
well versed in the art of lovemaking. Just when he was
about to explode inside her, he slid her back to the head
of his cock and held her there, both of them trembling
and kissing, entangling their tongues, until the threat of
climax had receded.

Then he pulled entirely out of her, gentled her forward onto the bed, holding her up on her knees. She
trembled with weakness, sweating, nearly sobbing with
need. When she'd rested her head on the pillow, snug-
gling one cheek hard against it and squeezing her eyes
closed while stretching her lips back from her teeth, he
guided his throbbing, jutting shaft into her from behind.

Holding her by the hips, he started thrusting, slowly
at first, the leather bedsprings wheezing softly. Gradually, he increased his speed until he was hammering
against her and she was by turns laughing ecstatically
and screaming horrifically, her thick, honey gold hair
flopping across her slender back and shoulders like the
mane of a love-frenzied mare.

When his seed burst from the head of his swollen cock to careen deep inside her, she turned her head forward and lifted her chin from the pillow, arching her back, every muscle tensing as she groaned from the depths of her throat.

Longarm held her taut against him, his own body convulsing as he skewered her, his head thrown back on his shoulders. Her legs and hips shook with convulsing, gradually dwindling spasms. He grunted savagely, gritting his teeth, until the final throes of his passion had come and gone.

Then he fell forward to collapse onto her back, resting his face against her neck, feeling his shaft dwindling inside her, tingling but spent.

Light still shone in the window—a wan, early evening glow—but he slid down beside her, wrapping his arms around her waist and cupping her breasts in his hands, and they slept like two exhausted nomads after crossing a vast desert.

Longarm woke first to some soft, green light lingering in the cloudless sky beyond the sashed window of the bedroom that, he assumed, Dalia had once shared with Tin Cup Pete. He slid quietly out of bed and pulled on only his whipcord trousers over his naked body; it was hot in the upstairs room and he still felt the heat from their frenzied coupling.

He grabbed a cigar and a lucifer match and, barefoot and bare-chested, he went downstairs and stood out on the porch to smoke the cigar and enjoy the caress of the cool sage-and-pine-scented breeze against his sweaty chest. On the far ridge, evening shadows mingled with the gold-brushed pines, and the evening wind and the several branching creeks around the ranch were a steady whisper.

Far off, an unseen eagle screeched.

Longarm felt too dreamy and sated—fulfilled in a way he'd rarely known before—to think about what had brought him there. The questions he had for the woman would all come tumbling back to him in their proper time.

He heard footsteps on the stairs and glanced over his shoulder to see Dalia step out onto the porch behind him. She'd brushed her long blond hair back from her face, and in the fading light it shone like gold glinting at the bottom of an alpine stream. She smiled sweetly as she wrapped a man's red and black checked robe over his shoulders, knowing that it got cold fast out here when the sun dropped behind the ridges.

Then she moved up beside him, and he could see the hunger still in her eyes. He set his cigar on the pine rail, took her in one arm, drew her to him brusquely, and kissed her.

She, too, wore a robe, but it came apart as she ground against him, and pulling his head away from hers, he looked down and saw the two ripe orbs touching his chest. The hunger for this rustic, beautiful, erotic woman returned with a vengeance, pushing against her.

He reached for her again, his heart thudding, but she laughed huskily and pulled away. Letting her robe hang open, the heavy breasts sloping with their jutting nipples, she smiled up at him obliquely while she slowly dropped to her knees before him, opening his trousers and sliding them down his thighs.

She placed her hands against his butt and closed her

mouth over his cock. With a grunt, he pressed his back against the porch rail and ground his feet into the floor.

"Now, then, where were we?" she said later, when they both lay in their robes on the thick, braided rug before the popping fire.

The mountain night had closed like a black glove, and the fire was the only light in the cabin. They lay facing each other, each propped on one elbow, sipping Longarm's Maryland rye from jelly jars.

"What's that?" Longarm said drowsily.

"Before we were so wantonly interrupted, you were about to get down to brass tacks."

"Oh, that," he said, taking a sip of the rye. "That can wait till morning."

She reached out and smoothed his thick, brown hair away from his eye. "Let's get it out of the way, Custis. I'm hiding nothing. No money, no secrets of any kind. All I have here is a few horses, one milk cow, and a few beeves I've managed to save from the ravages of another winter."

"Seems unlikely, don't it?" Longarm grunted. "Why would your husband go to the work of robbing the stage so you could keep the ranch, then not tell you where he hid the loot?"

"That puzzled me for a while, too. You see, I visited Pete in jail after he'd turned himself in after shooting the shotgun messenger. That was an accident, you know. Pete had never killed anything in his life but game. He wasn't himself that whole last year of his life. He was a desperate, confounded man, drinking heavily, and he never told me of his intentions to rob the stage. That day he was nervous, and his finger just slipped back against the trigger."

She squeezed her eyes closed as though suddenly, terribly pained. "Anyway, as I was saying, I visited him several times in jail while they were building the gallows, and he never told me where he hid the strongbox."

"Did you ask him?"

"Of course. He just said, 'In due time, Dalia.' "

"But that time never came."

"No, and I didn't continue to ask him. I thought maybe, just before they led him away to . . . be hung . . . he'd tell me." She swallowed and, squeezing her eyes closed again, a shiny wetness showing on her long, brown lashes, she shook her head as though waging a war against the memories. "But he didn't."

"Why would that be?"

"You know, I think he intended to," she said, opening her eyes and looking boldly up at Longarm again, though her voice owned the raspiness of suppressed emotion. "But I think, during all those days he spent in the jail, he came to realize deep down that I could never benefit from that stolen loot. He knew that I could never spend it here in town or anywhere else. He knew how the guilt over spending stolen blood money would rack me. This might be hard to believe after today, but I was raised a staunch Catholic, Custis. My father was a poor freighter, but no matter how deep in the mountains we were, he took my mother and me every Sunday to Mass. And if no priest was within a day's ride, he said Mass himself, then begged forgiveness for impersonating a man of the cloth."

Longarm flicked ashes into the fire and puffed his cigar, staring at the leaping flames with a confounded expression in his eyes.

"I know what you're thinking," Dalia said. "You want to believe me. On the other hand, maybe all that just happened here this afternoon was a ploy to *get* you to believe me." Her eyes sparkled in the firelight. "You *have* to believe me, Custis, I've never felt such a strong, honest urge in my life. My motivation for making love with you was pure . . . if not all that innocent. I'll be making my way over Cottonwood Pass to see Father Vincent in Buena Vista about this soon."

She set her hand on his forearm and squeezed. "But it had nothing to do with trying to shake you off my trail. Where Pete buried that strongbox is as big a mystery to me as anyone else. And if someone's going to find it, I wish they'd just go ahead and find it and leave me alone. I want no part of it."

Longarm sighed and placed his hand over hers on his forearm, believing her and hoping he was doing his believing with his brain and not his sundry parts down under. "Wouldn't be much point in him tellin' no one, would there? If he didn't tell you, who *would* he have told?"

"I honestly believe he intended to tell me right up until they dropped him off that scaffold." She shook her head and pursed her lips. "And because he couldn't decide if I'd turn the money in to the bank he stole it from or ruin my life by spending it, he just couldn't do it. He died at the end of the rope as thoroughly confounded as the rest of us now are."

"You must have some idea where he *might* have hidden it."

"It's a big country, and Pete was one of the first ones here. He knew all its secret hiding places better than anyone. Hell, that strongbox could be buried right here at the ranch or in one of the thirty draws that bleed into this valley, or on one of Pete's old claims. Might be buried back of Marshal Dobie's privy. That'd be like Pete. He had a wry sense of humor even about serious matters."

"You loved him, didn't you?"

"Yes, I did. He wasn't a handsome man, but he was devoted to me. He raised me up from a girl, and he made me laugh and feel like a woman."

She smiled whimsically and snuggled closer to Longarm, wrapping her leg over his.

"Are you forgetting Father Vincent?" Longarm said, lowering his head to smell her hair.

"My husband killed a man and stole money for me, Custis." She kissed him lightly on the lips and drew her leg tighter around his. "Give me another little taste of heaven—won't you? It's probably the only one I'll get."

Chapter 9

At nine o'clock the next morning, with the sun vaulting the toothy, snow-mantled ridges of the Great Divide in the east, rolling shadows down the cool, spruce green ridges below, Longarm halted Duke on a knoll and hipped around to stare back toward the Duchaine ranch behind him. Dalia was still there, standing about twenty yards in front of her cabin, shading her eyes with a hand as she stared toward him, her long skirts fluttering about her legs, her gold-blond hair fairly glowing.

A pang of loneliness pinched Longarm. The feeling was not for himself this time, but for her—a woman all alone out here, fending for herself while men scoured the mountains and canyons all around her for her husband's stolen loot. For a woman with Dalia Duchaine's natural desires, which Longarm had been fortunate enough to get to know rather well over the past twelve hours, life out here, as beautiful as the landscape was, had to be like solitary confinement in some remote desert prison.

He gave a wave, which she did not return, only con-

tinuing to stare toward him, shading her eyes. Turning
forward, he nudged Duke ahead with his boot heels. The
lunch sack she'd packed for him—two thick sandwiches
of roasted venison and wild onions with a dollop each of
her homemade mustard—jostled in front of his thigh
from the cord looped over his saddle horn.

At the east edge of the valley, he abandoned the trail
he'd followed in, swerving southward to follow a frothy
creek up through cool woods over a high divide. He
hadn't told Dalia he was lighting out to investigate the
scene of Marshal Lewis's murder. Every organ in his
body wanted to believe that she did not know where the
stolen money was—and one organ in particular—but his
bones were telling him to keep a cool, professional head.
As beautiful as Dalia Duchaine was, and as adept at man
pleasing, he knew from his own experience that deep
down she was tough as nails and hard as rocks.

Her not knowing where her husband had hidden the
strongbox that he'd gone to all the work of stealing just
for her didn't ooze a drop of liquid logic.

"No, Duke," the lawman said, scowling and moving
with the horse's pitch and sway as they followed the
slope through slow-to-leaf aspens into the next valley,
"that dog just don't hunt. And I sure would hate to get
myself buffaloed . . . not to mention back-shot . . . because I took the word of a brown-eyed beauty who
hauled my ashes right well and then some—scoured the
ole fire bin right down to its warped metal box, if'n you
get my drift."

He'd thought Dobie's map was fairly detailed, but
compared to this vast country teeming with an entirely
different landscape on the other side of every divide and

watershed, it was merely a few scratch marks on paper. When Longarm had ridden for two hours, figuring he was heading for Tin Cup Pete's first mine claim at Mirror Lake, he halted Duke suddenly at the top of a high divide. He looked around, frowning, the hair on his arms beginning to rise and his heart pattering with even more persistence than that caused by the altitude.

He'd been lost before in the Colorado Rockies. Not many men who'd ventured into that vast, rugged terrain had not had that eerie realization—that slight hiccup and stiffening of the spine and leg muscles—that comes only moments before icy tremors of panic roll through the blood like miniature tidal waves. And while he'd never been so badly lost that he hadn't finally been able to ride himself back to getting found again, the feeling was not a good one. Here, he had nothing to compare the map to but trees—an endless expanse of narrow pine bowls nearly blocking out the sun in some places, sloping this way and rising in that direction.

Making matters worse, the sun *itself* was not where he felt it should be if he were heading in the right direction. A man could spend a lot of time out here, fending off grizzlies and bobcats and riding his horse into the ground, trying to find his way to where he'd *thought* he was going.

Longarm took a deep, calming breath, then gigged Duke forward. The sick, light-headed feeling did not leave him for nearly forty-five minutes, until he'd rounded the shoulder of a mountain and stared down to where a creek drummed from a long, high, rocky pass into a sky blue pond nestled at the bottom of a rocky, pine-sheathed canyon.

Longarm looked at the map, then at the lake.

Mirror Lake. Had to be, judging by the formations that Dobie had scratched around its signifying circle on the map. Somehow, in spite of himself, Longarm had found it.

Relief washed over him as keenly as the near-panic had done, and he gigged Duke down off the slope and stopped him beside the bubbling, churning stream. He looked around as the horse lowered its head to drink from a small back-eddy, twitching its ears at the creek's steady, chugging rush. An old trail followed the east side of the lake, not much more than a narrow ledge between the lake and the steep, boulder-strewn, pitted and slashed ridge rising several thousand feet toward the sky.

Several troughs had been washed into the side of the ridge over the eons, and one such ridge had obviously spilled an avalanche—now only about fifty yards of dirty, slowly melting snow—onto the lake. The snow-bank was about twenty yards across, and when Duke had had his fill of the refreshing snowmelt, Longarm stepped down from the saddle. He, too, took a drink of the water, which was so icy he thought he could feel his molars crack, then led the horse across the snowbank to the other side and along the lake's east side, heading north.

There was a cut carved into the side of the eastern ridge, the mouth of which was hidden by rocks and smaller snowbanks. Longarm didn't see it until he was nearly even with it. The narrow, jagged defile led into the ridge for a hundred feet before it doglegged to the left.

"Nice place for a claim, if you ask me," Longarm said, brushing the back of a gloved hand across his windburned cheek.

Duke snorted and swished his tail.

Longarm glanced at the horse with reproof. "Don't tell me you don't like box canyons neither. Come on, you owly son of a bitch!"

After he'd tugged on the horse's reins a couple of times, Duke snorted and allowed himself to be led into the rocky defile that was still choked here and there with snow. Little rivers of mud ran between the snowbanks, and a couple of times the mud nearly sucked Longarm's boots off. He saw plenty of coyote and fox tracks, and atop one snowbank was a pile of scat threaded with deer fur that he recognized as mountain lion.

The dogleg led into a wider part of the canyon that dead-ended fifty yards farther on, choked with boulders fallen from the higher reaches. In the box canyon's left wall, a notch appeared—an alcove of sorts that appeared to have been chipped out of the rock with man-made tools.

Longarm walked up to the notch and peered inside, his upper lip and his mustache lifting a wry smile. The smile faded when he saw that the padlock on the stout log door filling the gap, framed in heavy timbers, had a bullet through its stout iron middle, and that the locking bolt hung free.

He reached forward and pushed the door open. It caught on something inside. Longarm leaned his weight against it, and shoved it open farther, bunching his lips with exertion as he scraped a rock or something else as heavy across the floor behind it. When he got the door as far open as its rusty, steel hinges would allow, he stepped inside, having to duck his head, cautiously inspecting the rotting door frame and the mine's pitted ceiling to make sure nothing was about to cave in.

He took another step inside, staying within the brassy light pushing in from behind him, and looked around. It was a typical mine portal, as far as he could tell—a narrow corridor carved out of the rock and smelling like trapped air, rocks, mice droppings, and bat guano. Moisture glistened along one of the ceiling beams.

Ahead, the mine tunnel led back into inky darkness. He saw no reason to probe it. The ruined padlock meant someone else had been here. Had Lewis shot the lock after he'd gotten the tip about Tin Cup Pete's old claim and come to look for the strongbox?

The question had barely brushed through Longarm's puzzled brain when his straying gaze stopped suddenly on the floor at the base of the mine opening's right wall, about ten feet from the door. He went over and hunkered on his haunches, running a gloved finger along the rectangular lines pressed into the mine's packed dirt floor. The lines traced the shape of a box roughly three feet long by two feet wide, and heavy enough to have flattened the dirt beneath it.

The strongbox had been here, all right. Tin Cup Pete must have cached it here. But who had found it?

Had Pete moved it, perhaps having decided this old mining claim wasn't such a great hiding place after all? Or had someone else moved it—someone Pete had told?

Marshal Lewis had been shot around a month ago, when he'd come up here to investigate the shaft. At that time, this cut would have still been filled with snow, and he wouldn't have been able to get in here. Someone had shot him anyway. Likely believing the marshal was on a hot trail, the shooter had wanted to make sure he, the shooter, got to the loot before the marshal did.

Was it the shooter then who'd come back later, when the snow had melted from the cut, and retrieved the loot?

Longarm sucked in a deep breath, brushed his hand across his mustache, and cast his gaze around the musty, shadowy mine portal, hearing the faint drip of water—probably snowmelt from above—deep inside the dark shaft. There was also the faint but distinguishable sound of a rat.

If anyone had found the loot, they likely would have left the country in a hurry. Not many men—or women—had the patience to sit on a cache that size for any length of time before the notion of spending it got the better of them. And anyone waving a sizable chunk of money around these parts might as well scream: "I found it! I found it!" The stage company responsible for the money would be on them like a duck on a June bug.

But anyone suddenly leaving the Tin Cup country would attract nearly as much suspicion.

So, if the loot had been discovered by anyone with an ounce of sense, they'd sit on it until the dust around the search for the loot finally settled. Which meant it was likely still around these parts . . . somewhere . . .

Where? Who had discovered it here and moved it?

Marshal Lewis had likely been shot by someone other than the thief who'd nabbed the strongbox, as the box had to have been taken either last fall, before the snows had socked in this canyon, or after the snow had melted, probably only a week or two ago. Maybe the thief had been put on the loot's scent by the inquiring marshal himself.

"Back to square fuggin' one," Longarm sighed.

He rose and moved to the open door. Pensively staring into the small, sunlit box canyon, his mind on the problem at hand, he reached inside his shirt pocket for a cigar. Nothing like a smoke to oil the brain pistons.

Duke stood where Longarm had ground-tied him, but the horse was looking around warily, lifting first one hoof and then the next, fidgeting.

"What's the matter with you, hoss?" Longarm said as he bit the end off a nickel cheroot. He spat the paper into the mud before him, and chuckled. "See a mouse?"

Something tore into Longarm's upper arm with a sudden, searing, tooth-gnashing pain, puffing dust from his coat and throwing the lawman back inside the portal. Snarling, he dropped the cigar and clawed at the entrance timbers, but raked them only with his fingertips before hitting the ground on his butt.

The crack of the rifle that had shot him echoed demonically around the canyon. Duke screamed. Shod hooves thundered as the horse galloped out of the cut.

Someone squealed, *"I got him! I got him!"*

Chapter 10

Another bullet slammed into the ground where Longarm had been standing before the first shot had torn through his arm and thrown him back inside the cave. Dust and rock shards peppered his face.

Outside, someone whooped and hollered as another rifle boomed and another slug tore slivers from the side of the old timbered door frame.

"You're dead, lawdog—y'hear?" another man hollered at the top of his lungs. *"Dead!"*

Cradling his wounded arm and snarling furiously—bushwhacked again!—Longarm rolled to his left as three more bullets, fired almost simultaneously, pelted the door frame and the floor just inside the entrance. Quickly, the lawman ripped off his neckerchief and wrapped it tightly over the wound from which blood pumped redly, soaking his shirt and claw hammer coat.

"You think he's dead?" one of the shooters asked another.

"He rolled away from the door, so it's my guess he's still kickin'," said another.

A slightly higher-pitched male voice yelled, "That was some heart shot, Willie! Looks to me like you got him in the arm, ye damn fool!"

"Go diddle your mother, Lewis," someone said with a chuckle, adding, "'less you're gettin' tired o' the same ol', same ol'!"

One of the other men laughed and triggered a rifle, the bullet ricocheting off a rock just outside the mine entrance and buzzing down the yawning blackness of the corridor beyond Longarm, where it struck something with a muffled ping.

Longarm grimaced at the throbbing pain in his arm.

Before he'd rolled away from the door, he'd seen a smoke puff on the canyon's lip, twelve feet above the canyon floor and slightly to the left, between two granite boulders. All three bushwhackers were likely up there, shooting into the canyon.

When the lawman had knotted the neckerchief tight around his arm, he slipped his double-action .44 from its cross-draw holster and thumbed back the hammer. He crawled to the rock wall just left of the door and, as more shots hammered the front of the mine entrance and the ground in front of it, he climbed to his feet and sidled over toward the door, through which sunlit dust wafted.

Bowing his head slightly beneath the low ceiling and pressing his back to the rock wall, he waited as the shooters continued shooting intermittently and yelling Southern-accented taunts.

One of the bushwhackers yelled, "Hold on, hold on! We're just wasting ammo!"

A couple more bullets hammered the mine entrance. Then the gunfire stopped, and the echoes fell silent.

In the canyon, the wind soughed. Dust swirled beyond the open front door. Some gravel loosed by the
shooters rattled down the canyon wall.

"Hey, lawdog!" one of the bushwhackers shouted.

Longarm winced as another pain spasm hammered
up and down his wounded arm. He cleared his throat
and turned toward the door with a savage scowl. "What
the hell do you want, dead man?"

Silence.

Someone laughed and said just loudly enough for
Longarm to hear, "What's that? What'd he call me?"

Longarm bounded forward and out the doorway,
aiming at a head jutting between the two boulders he'd
seen before, and fired. The bushwhacker between the
boulders hadn't even started turning away from his
compadre before Longarm's .44 slug crashed through
the side of the man's shabby, feather-trimmed derby hat.
The man's head jerked as Longarm dropped to a knee
and took hasty aim at the second man atop the canyon's
lip, who'd turned toward Longarm, dropping his lower
jaw in shock.

The lawman's slug punched through the man's left
shoulder. As the man screamed, pitched back, bounced
off a rock behind him, and slumped forward over the
canyon's lip, Longarm drew a quick but steady bead on
the third shooter. He fired just as the man—a kid really,
and an ugly kid at that, in a rat-hair coat and a checked
bowler hat—gave a terrified, girlish shriek and threw
himself sideways.

Longarm's bullet spanged off a rock where the kid's
open mouth had been a quarter second before.

The kid crawled off down the ridge and scrambled to

his feet as Longarm fired another round that blew up rocks and gravel at the kid's flying heels. The lawman was about to fire another shot, when the kid disappeared down the grade toward the lake and out of view of the canyon.

Longarm dropped his gaze to where the second man he'd shot was rolling down the ridge, grunting and groaning. He hit the canyon floor, yelling, "Ah, *gawddamnit*!"

He was a tall, bearded hombre with pinched-up, crazy eyes and wearing a Confederate greatcoat so old that the stripes had faded off the sleeves and the Rebel gray was nearly white. The coat hung open to reveal the man's ratty work shirt, filthy duck trousers held up with suspenders, and knee-high, lace-up boots favored by miners and gandy dancers.

Longarm aimed his Colt at the man and climbed to his feet. At the same time, the bushwhacker scrambled to his own feet and, picking up a squash-sized hunk of black granite, ran toward Longarm with white-ringed, crazy eyes spitting fire and cocking his arm low and back behind his shoulder for a killing blow with the rock. His bald, hatless head glistened in the sunlight, his boots clomped, and his greatcoat blew out behind him in the wind.

Longarm spread his feet and held the Colt half out from his side, the hammer cocked. A skeptical sneer twisted his lips as he waited to see if the man would stop.

The man didn't stop.

POW! POW!

Dust blew from around the man's chest as Longarm's

slugs split his breastbone, one beneath the other in a straight line. The man slowed his pace until, lowering the rock to his side, he staggered a few more feet toward Longarm before dropping to both knees.

The rock fell from his fingers. He glared up at Longarm. His lids grew heavy.

Eyes rolling back into their sockets, he fell in the dirt and expired with a long, loud fart.

Longarm walked up to him and stared down. "Fool."

Bunching his lips against the pain in the arm while reloading his Colt, he jogged back down the canyon. He flicked the loading gate closed and spun the cylinder as he bounded out of the canyon mouth, the crystal-clear, half-frozen lake yawning before him.

Hoof thuds sounded to his left, and he turned to see the ugly kid galloping along the shelf between the ridge and the lake, hazing two riderless horses out ahead of him. As the kid put his claybank onto the melting avalanche, Longarm started to raise his Colt. A nicker sounded to his right.

He wheeled to see Duke standing twenty feet away, reins drooping. Beyond, the remains of another avalanche blocked the trail. The skittish horse must have been too owly to flounder through the dirty snow of his own accord, and had chosen to stand here instead, shivering.

Longarm dropped his Colt into its holster, ran to the horse, and shucked his Winchester. Racking a shell into the breech, he ran back to the canyon mouth. Having crossed the rushing creek, the ugly kid was galloping around the far side of the lake now, the other two horses scattering into the trees ahead of him. He had his head down, and he was flapping his arms like wings.

Longarm snapped the rifle to his shoulder, tracked the kid, and fired.

The bullet blew up a clump of mud from the grassy slope on the other side of the kid. The kid flinched as the rifle's whip-crack reached his ears and echoed flatly across the lake.

Longarm ejected the smoking cartridge, seated fresh, and fired again.

The kid's horse had just turned to follow a trail up the mountain through the pines when the kid slumped forward, dropping his right shoulder. The horse and the kid disappeared behind a patch of willows, and when the horse emerged, the kid was not in the saddle.

Longarm lowered the Winchester, ejected the spent cartridge onto the rocks around his boots, and levered a fresh shell into the chamber before off-cocking the hammer.

He staggered back as fatigue and nausea from the wound washed through him. He sat on a rock and glanced at the neckerchief glistening with fresh blood. With a curse, and casting a scowl toward where the kid had fallen in the willows, he leaned the rifle against the rocky bank. He gently removed the neckerchief from the wound, then shrugged out of his coat and carefully cut off the sleeve of his pin-striped shirt, about four inches above the wound, with his folding barlow knife.

Heaving himself to his feet, he walked over to the shore of the lake, dropped to his knees, and bent low to bathe his upper arm in the frigid snowmelt. He sucked a sharp breath as his muscles contracted against the bone-splintering, heart-stopping chill.

His heart quickened its beat as if in protest at the icy

assault, but he held his shoulder low, keeping his arm submerged, until the snowmelt had numbed the pain to a muffled throb and the blood had finished ribboning out away from the wound in the water that had to have been only a degree or two from freezing.

Straightening and lifting his arm from the lake, Longarm inspected the wound—a ragged, .45-caliber hole across the outside of his muscled arm four inches above the elbow. He already knew the bullet hadn't hit the bone; if it had, he'd be rolling around on the ground in much worse pain than he was. It was a flesh wound—a deep one, but a flesh wound just the same, with an entrance and exit hole.

He wrung his neckerchief out in the lake, draped it over a rock, then staggered over to where Duke stood before the far snowbank, regarding Longarm warily, twitching his ears and sidling away.

"Easy, boy," Longarm grunted. "Shootin's done for now."

Longarm produced his bottle of Maryland rye from his saddlebags, removed the cork with his teeth, and took several long pulls, his Adam's apple bobbing in his thick, brown neck.

The smooth rye washed through him, conspiring with the cold water to numb the pain in the arm further, to take the general edge from the current nettling circumstance, and to paint the lake in the soft hues of semi-inebriation.

Longarm held the bottle up above his head, stretching his lips back from his teeth and shaking his head with reluctance. "Dear Jesus," he beseeched, "please forgive me for the waste of such good elixir, but I reckon I don't have no trade whiskey or Apache *tizwin* just now."

With that, he poked the lip of the bottle into the wound and dropped it. The rye shot into the fresh hole like liquid fire, turning Longarm's knees to putty and nearly stopping his heart.

"Jesus!"

His knuckles buckled, and he sagged against the horse. He raised the bottle once more and tightened his jaws against the red fire washing through his body all the way to his soul.

Lowering the bottle, he had to fight to keep his knees straight as he stared out at the lake, clenching his jaws and waiting for surcease from the searing misery shooting up and down his arm, through his chest and belly, and across both hips and into his thighs.

After what seemed a good week and a half, but was probably only thirty seconds or so, the pain dwindled to a muted throb, and Longarm took another pull from the bottle before corking it and returning it to his saddlebags. Then he wrapped the soaked neckerchief, nearly as cold as the lake water, across the cleaned-out wound, and shrugged into his coat.

"Let's go bag our meat, Duke," he grunted as, holding his arm tenderly across his belly, he heaved himself into his saddle.

He booted the horse along the lakeside trail and over the avalanche and the tumbling creek. When he rose up the mountain through the willows, he found the kid crouched over a small boulder, his trembling, bloody back facing Longarm.

The lawman held his .44 in his hand as the kid, hearing Duke's hooves above the rushing of the stream below, turned suddenly toward him, bringing up a big Colt

Dragoon horse pistol in his left hand. He grunted as he wrestled himself around to face the lawman, spitting, "Ya . . . ya kilt me, ya big son of a bitch!"

He'd lost his hat, and his thin, yellow hair curled around his head. He had ears the size of most men's hands, and a jutting, spade-shaped chin, enhancing the wide spread of his weird blue eyes. Glistening sweat beads dribbled down from his forehead.

"Not yet," Longarm said, caressing the Colt's trigger. "But if you don't drop that hogleg, I will."

Chapter 11

The kid narrowed his crazy eyes, appearing to consider his options, then tossed the big Dragoon into the brush. He slumped forward, pressing his hand to his bloody upper right chest, and his bottom lip swelled and trembled as he sobbed, "Ah, Jesus—it *hurts!*"

"Don't it?"

"I ain't never been shot before!"

"You'll get used to it," Longarm said, swinging down from his saddle and dropping Duke's reins in the brush.

"Yessir, ya kilt me, ya son of a bitch," the kid continued, tipping his head back on his shoulders, slitting his eyes, and showing a gap-toothed wince. "Just like ya done Uncle Ralph and Bubba T."

"Like I said, not yet," Longarm growled, standing over the kid, holding his pistol down by his thigh, and fisting his other hand till the knuckles turned white. "But it wouldn't be anything you didn't deserve, you scrawny, yellow-gutted little bushwhacker. By rights, I oughta kick you around the lake, tie a rock around your neck, and toss you in. The only reason I don't is because I wouldn't want to pollute such a pretty pond with the likes of an inbred little scoundrel like yourself."

"Add insult to injury, will ya?"

"What'd you bushwhack me for, you dumb little hill-billy?"

The kid bunched his lips and stared up at Longarm, his lower lip continuing to tremble, but now with as much rage as hurt and fear. "'Cause you ain't got no cause comin' around here, stickin' your damn nose where it don't belong. That stage loot is none of your business. It's *our* business—us folks with claims all around this country. We'll decide who finds it and keeps it!"

Longarm stared at the kid, his face implacable, his eyes incredulous.

"We heard who you was in town," the kid continued. "And we don't need no federal lawdog snoopin' around. Like my brother Bubba T. said—this is a local affair and it ain't no business of the bigwigs in Washington City!"

"That's the word goin' around town, huh? You all figure that stolen loot's as good as a high-grade mine claim? First one who finds it gets to keep it?"

The kid didn't say anything, but the anwer to Longarm's question was plain on his face.

Longarm chuckled without mirth. "Sonny, you're too fuckin' stupid to argue with."

The kid opened his mouth to retort, but before he could get the words out, Longarm said, "Shut up. Pull your hand away from that wound, let me see how bad it is." He shot the little bushwhacking privy snipe a wry glance. "'Lessen it's none of my business, that is."

Willie looked around stupidly. "Reckon there ain't no one else around to help me outta my tight spot." Wincing, he removed his hand from his shoulder. Blood seeped through the cloth of his rat-hair coat.

Longarm pulled the coat flap open, revealing the kid's bloody linsey-woolsey tunic with a V neck held together with whang strings. Longarm must have given a pained expression, because the kid made a high-pitched sound through his nose and said thinly, "Oh, Lord—am I gonna die? Should I be prayin'?"

"Couldn't hurt."

"Oh, Jesus . . ." The kid kicked his boots miserably.

"Don't go spasming around or you'll bleed out, ya fool kid. Where in the hell did you fellas cut my trail anyway?"

Sneering, the kid said, "We followed you to the widow's place. Figured she might tell you where the loot was hid. We was camped nearby the whole damn time."

Longarm's cheeks warmed with embarrassment. "You followed me all the way from Tin Cup?"

"Hope you enjoyed that blow job the widow give ya on the front porch!"

"Why, you little . . . !" Longarm cocked a boot to kick the kid, but stopped himself. "How in the hell didn't I see you?"

"Ralph and Bubba T.—they're damn good shadowers," the kid said proudly. Then the light in his eyes dimmed, and he sniffed. "At least, they were."

Longarm grumbled, abashed. "I'll see if I can find your horse, and then I'll get you to town . . . get us *both* to a sawbones, though why I don't drill a bullet through your forehead and throw you in the lake, I have no idea." He turned, grabbed Duke's reins, and started walking away, grumbling, "It'd be a lot less paperwork . . ."

He'd taken three steps when, a thought occurring to him, he stopped and turned back to Willie, who was moaning and groaning with his back against the rock. "Say, you don't know a bushwhacker named Yancy Carruthers, do you?"

The kid scowled up at Longarm. "Never heard of no Yancy Carruthers. Why should I?"

"I don't know," Longarm said, turning and climbing the trail through the pines. "Thought maybe you yellow-gutted bushwhackers hung together, that's all."

Longarm wasn't about to waste his good Maryland rye on the bushwhacking little snake whose full name he learned—on the long pull back to Tin Cup through several canyons gushing with creeks and freshets—was Willie Hobbs from Tunnel Hill, Georgia. Hobbs and his uncle and brother, now deceased, had come out here via Cripple Creek looking for their own private fortunes.

"And now Ralph and Bubba T. are both dead and I'm halfway there!" the kid sobbed, riding his claybank behind Longarm, who had tied the boy's hands to his saddle horn though it wasn't likely, with that ruined shoulder, he'd be doing much running.

"Ah, shut up," Longarm grumbled for the fifth or sixth time during the ride.

His own shoulder grieved him plenty, and the neckerchief he'd wrapped around the wound was blood-soaked, with blood leaking down the inside of his coat sleeve, by the time they twisted and climbed up the trail into the east edge of Tin Cup.

The town wasn't much busier than it had been when Longarm had arrived the day before. Only a handful of prospectors panned the willow-stippled beaver meadows that ran along the town's southern edge, between the town and a high, pine-studded ridge, and curved around the town's west edge to play out in a narrow canyon. White canvas tents flapped in the breeze along the meadows, no smoke issuing from their chimney pipes or from the stone fire rings near their front door flaps. Most of the long sluice boxes snaking from the creek banks to the streams, known as Long Toms, stood high and dry on their rickety pine stilts.

A few men were working their claims, spilling gravel into the sluice boxes or working with pick and shovel along the streambeds, slogging through the willow bogs. They were old-timers mostly. The younger men who didn't want to work so hard for their own El Dorados were likely off searching for the mysterious, coveted strongbox stolen by Tin Cup Pete Duchaine.

"Fools," Longarm muttered as he aimed the buckskin toward the small marshal's office.

"Is that all you can do—call me names?" the kid yelled indignantly from behind.

"Shut up, Willie." Longarm pulled Duke up to one of the two hitch racks fronting the jailhouse and climbed wearily down from his saddle. "The other thing I can do is toss your ass in the hoosegow and throw away the key, and I'm about to do just that."

He racked his bridle reins and started toward Willie's horse as the jailhouse door scraped open and Chester

Dobie appeared, blinking, his hair mussed as though he'd just awakened from a nap. He shuttled his narrowed eyes between Longarm and the kid.

"What have we here?"

"The kid bushwhacked me," Longarm said. "Turn the key on him, will you, Marshal? I'll file the charges later. I'm gonna go get sewed up if you have a sawbones hereabouts."

"Of course we got a sawbones," Dobie said, moving down off the jailhouse porch and glancing with concern at the bloody sleeve of Longarm's coat. He canted his head toward the jailhouse. "Straight back. Name's Soggy Wilson."

Longarm looked at the marshal skeptically.

"Soggy used to be a camp cook," Dobie said as he continued toward Willie Hobbs slouching in his saddle, chin dipped nearly to his chest. "Got tired of that and took to cleanin' out bullet wounds and settin' broken bones. Can't tell you if he got any *proper* training, but he's right handy at it. Last winter, I had a touch of the rheumatics in my shoulder, got so bad I couldn't sleep at night. Ole Soggy whipped me up some root powder that put that misery out in two days!"

"What about me?" the kid said as the marshal cut his hands loose of his saddle horn.

"I'll send Soggy over to see about you after he's done with me," Longarm grumbled and, holding his aching arm stiffly at his side, lit a cheroot and started humping around the jailhouse.

"Don't worry about your hoss, Marshal," Dobie called, grunting as he helped the kid out of his saddle.

"I'll have Pedro Estevan take your horse over to the livery barn."

"Obliged," Longarm grunted, firing a lucifer on his belt buckle and touching the flame to his nickel cheroot, and strode around the side of the jailhouse. The inside of his coat sleeve, down to his wrist, was slimy with half-congealed blood that gave him a bone-penetrating chill made worse by the icy breeze blowing down from the piney northern slopes still capped with winter snows.

He needed a stiff shot of rye and a hot bath, both of which he'd tend to as soon as Soggy Wilson had seen to his arm, though he had to admit he didn't have much confidence in a pill roller named Soggy. He liked his medicos named George or William or Charles. Soggy? He might do just as well on his own with a bottle of whiskey and a roll of cotton bandages, but he had no bandages and it raked him to use good Maryland rye on the outside of his person when cheap, mining-camp rot-gut would serve the same purpose.

Soggy likely had both, as well as two hands to wrap the wound with.

He found the so-called medico cleaning a deer behind his shabby, sprawling cabin on the bank of Tin Cup Creek, at the south edge of the little town. Soggy was a man in his later middle years who predictably resembled a camp cook more than a medico, but he took one look at the federal lawman's arm and grunted, "Clean flesh wound. Shit. Ain't nothin' to clean that up. You'll be good as new in no time, if you ain't bled dry, that is. Go on upstairs and I'll be along just as soon as I finish carv-

ing out this buck's gall bladder. I'll boil it down for female complaints, and the ladies won't know it from that
fancy stuff they send from St. Louis!"

Longarm grumbled skeptically and started up the
outside staircase, heading for the cabin's second story.

"Put a pot o' coffee on while you're waitin', will
ya?" the doctor yelled. "I could sure do with a cup of
mud!"

Later, sipping coffee while Longarm sipped brandy
that the doctor kept around for medicinal purposes and
poured out by the thimbleful, Soggy Wilson cleaned the
lawman's arm like he'd been doing it all his life. He
used several different substances, one being red, the
other a murky blue, to clean both holes in Longarm's
upper arm, and Longarm didn't inquire about what they
were. Probably best if he didn't know.

Soggy Wilson was a little man with a pointy nose, a
gray spade beard, and thick muttonchop whiskers, who
breathed raspily as he worked, grunting and belching
from time to time with indigestion. He wore the attire of
the average gold panner, including a mashed-in canvas
hat and high-topped, lace-up boots. But Longarm was
impressed by how quickly and adeptly the man stitched
closed the entrance and exit wounds after cauterizing
them both carefully with a hot knife.

"I'm just gonna bandage this once today," the medico
said as a cuckoo clock ticked loudly on the cedar-paneled
wall of his makeshift examining room. "Tomorrow
morning, you take it off and leave it off. Air's the best
thing for fightin' infection." He leaned toward Longarm
and wrinkled an admonishing brow. "And go easy on the
hooch. It don't do nothin' but make you feel like skippin'

and hoppin' to the next rodeo, but it don't do that hole in your arm a damn bit of good."

"How could I do anything but go easy on it, the way you dole it out by the teaspoonful?" Longarm grouched as he sat atop a scarred wooden bench padded with deer hide.

"Scared o' the damn stuff myself. Where do you think I got the name Soggy? On account I used to be soggy all day every day with that busthead for about fifteen years!"

"What's your real name?"

"George."

"Figures."

"Why's that?"

"Forget it," Longarm said, throwing back the last of his thimbleful of hooch.

Soggy Wilson had just started wrapping the wound with gauze when boots clomped up the outside staircase and Chester Dobie came in. "How's the patient, Doc?"

"He'll live if he minds me about the hooch," the medico said as he worked.

To Longarm, Dobie said, "He give you the who-hit-John lecture?"

"Too much o' that and not enough hooch." Longarm winced as the old man wrapped the gauze tight around the tender wound. "How's the kid?" he asked the marshal.

"Loud." Dobie doffed his hat, sank into a Windsor chair by the door, and hiked a worn stockman's boot on his knee. "Any luck with Mrs. Duchaine?"

The tips of Longarm's ears warmed as he remembered his carnal shenanigans out at the Duchaine place.

"Nah. She's got me that far from believing she has no idea where Tin Cup Pete stashed the loot, though."

Dobie opened his mouth to speak, but a mule's bray from outside stopped him. Hooves clomped, and a dog started barking angrily.

"What the hell's that?" Dobie said, rising from his chair and angling a look out the door toward the front of the two-story cabin.

"Soggy!" a man shouted in the distance. "Soggy, you in there?"

"Ah, shit," the medico said. "I thought I was gonna have an easy day, with the panners all off killing themselves in the canyons. Here I got an arm wound, a shoulder wound over to the jail, and now—"

"He's in here, Silas!" Dobie called out the door, waving his hat. Glancing over his shoulder at the doctor, who was just finishing up with Longarm, he said, "It's Silas Manduke. He's holdin' his arm like he broke it."

"Well, breaks is easy anyway," Soggy grumbled. "'Less the bone's all split up. If that's the case, it's easier just to lop the whole damn thing off and be done with it. But if I have to do that, I won't be playin' poker over to Jasper Boetticher's tent tonight, damn Silas's eyes!"

Outside, there rose the sound of a man breathing hard. Boots crunched grass and sage branches. "Soggy!"

"He's up here, Silas," Dobie said, still holding the door open and staring down the outside stairs. "What'd you do to yourself?"

"What the fuck's it look like I done to myself, Marshal?" the man snapped, clomping up the stairs. "I broke my fuckin' arm!"

"No call to get testy," Dobie said, holding the door open as a man no larger than Soggy Wilson stumbled into the room, pressing his left arm across his belly.

Silas Manduke wore coveralls and a denim jacket with suspenders showing beneath it, and his pewter-colored beard brushed against his big, brass belt buckle.

"No call to get testy, he says," the prospector huffed, crouching over his injured wing and grimacing. "My fuckin' mule throws me off her fuckin' back twenty miles from town, and the marshal tells me not to get *testy*!"

"What the hell were you doin' twenty miles from town, Silas?" said Soggy Wilson, crouching to give Longarm's injured appendage one last close scrutiny. "Your hole is up Curly Jim Draw, ain't it?"

Before the newcomer could respond, the medico glanced at Longarm. "You're ready, Marshal. Remove the wrap tomorrow, but keep that arm clean. Them Chinee girls over yonder'll likely clean your coat for you, but I'd say your shirt's a goner. Hang around while they clean your duds"—Soggy gave a lascivious wink—"and them Daughters o' Han'll have you forgettin' in no time you was shot. Next to me, they're the best medicos in town!"

Soggy wheezed a ribald laugh.

"Much obliged," Longarm said, hopping down off the examination table, "for the doctorin' *and* the advice."

He went over to where he'd dumped his shirt and coat on a bench near the doctor's rolltop desk. The marshal, who had retaken his seat in the Windsor chair and was spinning his hat on his boot toe, said to the broken-armed prospector gingerly claiming Longarm's spot on the examination table, "Where'd you say you were when Bessie unseated you, Silas?"

Manduke pinched his eyes and bunched his cheeks as Soggy began probing the man's arm, which was bulging above the elbow, with his fingers. "Grizzly Ridge. Years ago, me and Pete filed our first claim together up there, just under the ridgeline. Abandoned it before anyone else even started comin' up to these parts."

"What in Christ's name were you doing up there now?" Dobie asked, incredulous. "That's damn remote country."

Manduke swallowed and tipped his head back with a wince as Soggy now probed the grisly bulge in his arm with all ten fingertips. "My vein at Curly Jim Draw dropped down beneath a good-sized fist of solid granite and I couldn't pick at it no more—*Jesus Christ, Soggy, that hurts, damn you!*—so I decided to give me an' ole Pete's claim another shot."

"You don't say," Dobie said thoughtfully. "Sounds to me like you're wastin' your time up there, Silas. They say there's no gold up thataway. And you ain't as young as you used to be. You best stay closer to town."

"What am I s'posed to do—go crazy over that stage loot like the rest of the fuckin' jaspers around here?" Manduke scoffed. "Besides, Pete always said he had a feelin' we abandoned that claim too soon. Hell, maybe I'll find the mother lode and move into town and build me a big, Jay Gould-style lodge and drive them four-flushin' loot chasers crazy!"

He chuckled and groaned at the pain in his arm at the same time.

"Yep, you broke her good, Silas," Soggy said, backing away from the man, fists on his hips. "Ain't comin' through the skin, though, so you'll live to break rocks another day, I reckon."

"Someone's been ridin' around up there past couple weeks," Manduke said to Dobie as Soggy splashed brandy into a water glass. "Makin' all kinds o' tracks in the mud. Same rider. I recognized the silver-shaped flaw in the right rear hoof. I was followin' his most recent trail—might be a claim jumper, you know—when Bessie spooked at a bobcat and pitched me ass-over-teakettle. I hit the trail with one hell of a loud fuckin' *crack*! At first I thought I'd landed on a branch, but then I saw my poor fuckin' arm."

"Ouch," Dobie said.

Soggy held the brandy out to Manduke, who took it but continued talking to the marshal. "If someone's tryin' to jump that ole claim of me and Pete's, Dobie, he's gonna buy a bullet from me sure enough." He dropped his chin and rolled his eyes sincerely. "I wanna tell you first, so you know he's got it comin'."

Dobie grimaced. "Ah, shit, Silas, as if I don't have enough trouble with all these scalawags combing these—"

"If you two'll excuse me, I'd like to go ahead and do my business here so I can make my poker game tonight," Soggy Wilson said, interrupting the marshal. He took hold of the hand of Silas's broken arm, getting ready to jerk the broken bone into place. "If you two wanna palaver about killin' claim jumpers, do it on your own time!"

He glanced at the injured prospector. "Go ahead and

drink that brandy, damnit, Silas. I never seen ya hesitate with a glass in your hand before!"

Longarm, who had been listening closely to the conversation, especially the parts involving Tin Cup Pete, finished buttoning his vest over his otherwise naked torso and grabbed the last two and a half cheroots from the pocket of his ruined shirt. Gentling two cigars into a vest pocket and poking the half-smoked one into his mouth, he had his mind as much on that other mine as on the haggling between Soggy Wilson and Silas Manduke. When he'd grabbed his shirt and his coat, he clomped over to the door, and Marshal Dobie rose from his chair, staring at Longarm skeptically.

"What's on your mind, Marshal?" he asked as he followed Longarm down the outside stairs. "Don't think I've ever seen a man quite so deep in thought."

Just then, a crunching sounded from inside the office above, and Silas Manduke loosed a coyotelike howl.

Dobie winced and shook his head as he continued down the stairs behind Longarm. Longarm, barely registering the grisly sounds, glanced over his near-naked shoulder while puffing smoke around his cigar.

"Did you know about Tin Cup Pete's first mine claim, Dobie? I mean, the one before the one that *I* thought had been the first one and where Marshal Lewis was killed?"

"The one at Grizzly Ridge? Can't say as I did—no, sir," the marshal said. "Hell, he might have had more claims before that one even. Pete was an odd, secretive man."

Standing near the front of Soggy Wilson's cabin, Longarm flicked ashes from his cigar and nudged his hat brim up his forehead. "You think there's any chance Pete might have stashed the loot up there at Grizzly Ridge? Or barring that, that whoever took the loot from his claim at Mirror Lake stashed it up thataway?"

"Wait a minute," Dobie said, spreading his feet in front of Longarm and holding up his hands palms out. "How do you know the loot was hid at Mirror Lake? And how do you know it was moved?"

Longarm shivered as the cold, early evening wind blew over the bald, snow-mantled ridge. "Damn, it gets cold up here of a night. I tell you what—I'm gonna drop my coat off with those Chinese gals to have it sewed up and cleaned. Then I'm gonna fetch my spare shirt and my heavy coat from my saddlebags. While I'm doin' that, I'm gonna think it all through so I can speak more plain—if you get my drift. Why don't I meet you at a hop house in, say, twenty minutes?"

"All right." Dobie nodded. "The Busted Knuckle is right across from the Federated Livery. That's where I had Pedro take your horse. The saloon's a tent affair, but they serve right good ale, and that's all I drink these days."

"Meet you there."

The two men separated.

Longarm tossed his ruined shirt on Soggy's trash pile and made for the Chinese washhouse–whorehouse, puffing cigar smoke.

His brow was mantled with hard thought.

Chapter 12

Longarm was tempted to stay for the blow job offered by the rosy-cheeked Miss Columbine at the washhouse–whorehouse, but since he'd had one just last night and then another one that morning before he was fully awake—and because Marshal Dobie was waiting for him at the hop house—he politely declined and left his bloody frock in the Chinese girls' care.

He checked on his horse in the Federated Livery barn, and retrieved a clean shirt and his heavy buckskin mackinaw from his saddlebags and bedroll respectively. He also grabbed his Winchester; with all the treasure seekers who'd tried to take the government out of the game in a hail of hot lead, he'd likely need it.

Marshal Dobie was nursing a schooner of dark, frothy ale at one of the three occupied tables in the Busted Knuckle tent saloon. The place smelled like pine dust, spilled beer, wet canvas, and cheap tobacco. Longarm walked in, letting the tent flap drop down behind him. The apron, who was not wearing an apron but a bear coat stretched taut across his burly frame, was stacking tobacco pouches on a row of pine shelves behind the bar. As Longarm made his way to Dobie's table, he hollered for an ale.

"S'pose you want me to fetch it out there fer ye," the bartender said over his shoulder with a scowl.

"I'd appreciate it, friend," Longarm said, dragging out a pine-log stool and sitting down across from Dobie.

"Want me to drink it fer ya, too?"

"No, I'll drink it myself." Longarm relit his cheroot, puffing smoke. "But thanks for the offer just the same." To Dobie, smirking across the table from him, he said, "He always that friendly?"

"Smoke's been off his feed since his Ute squaw left him for a shifty-eyed Indian agent out of Glenwood Springs." Dobie flipped a dime onto the table scored with several sets of initials and tobacco burns. "First one's on me. In spite of Smoke's colicky demeanor, I think you'll find his ale right appealing. The best stout I've tasted this side of Indianapolis."

"Indianapolis?" Longarm said, removing the two-inch cheroot from his mouth and loosening his mackinaw sleeve around his freshly wrapped wound. "What were you doing there?"

"Being raised. My father was a schoolmaster, believe it or not."

"I didn't think you looked like rock-farming stock." Longarm glanced up at the burly apron, who set a frothy, coal black mug of aromatic stout onto the table, some of the coffee-colored suds dribbling down the side. "You're a gentleman and a scholar, friend."

Smoke growled and ambled back to his plank-board

bar stretched across beer casks. Turning to Dobie, Longarm said, "What brought you out here?"

"I had the crazy idea folks in mining camps would have the money as well as the hankering for fine furniture. That's what I made, starting when I went to work for Herman & Shelvin in Indianapolis. After learning the trade there, I set out on my own, kicked around a few cow and mining camps, and ended up here, flat broke and with a wife, who'd grown tired of my crazy furniture-making shit." Dobie shrugged. "She lit out for home, and I got the divorce notice in the mail six months later. I drank for a year, then crawled up out of a muddy gully to find a deputy marshal's star pinned to my chest."

"Like the job?"

"I did when it was quiet, and before Lewis was shot. I liked being a deputy a whole lot more than the head key twister. Never had much of a commanding presence, and I've never been good with a handgun. Mostly, for bar fights and whatnot, I use the backside of a shovel."

"Sounds right effective."

"Does a helluva business to a man's nose, and afterward he's usually mad you ruined his face, but grateful you didn't use a forty-five." Dobie took a deep sip of his ale, then wiped the froth from his clean-shaven mouth. "So, tell me, Marshal . . ."

"Custis'll do here."

"All right, tell me, Custis, what's this about the loot being moved?"

Longarm sipped his ale. Its bitterness was well cut by the hops, and the thick fluid stayed on his tongue to complement the cigar smoke he followed it with. He exhaled smoke through a weary, perplexed sigh, and said, "You probably weren't able to get into Tin Cup Pete's digging up to Mirror Lake because of the snow."

Dobie shook his head. "When Lewis was shot, that cut still had several feet left in it."

"That means Lewis didn't get into it either. But he suspected it was there. You have no idea why?"

"He didn't mention it to me. Probably just playing a hunch."

"Then we'll likely never know. Maybe he just knew about the mine and figured it would be a right nice place for Pete to stash his loot. Someone followed him and plunked him when they realized where he was headed, and wanted to get there first."

"Back-shot the poor old bastard," Dobie said with a scowl, lifting his schooner to his lips once more. "Problem is, any one of those yahoos out running around those mountains and draws right now could have done it. Just like that kid that plunked you."

"I hear you." Longarm scowled down at his beer. "Speaking of him . . ."

"Soggy knows where the cell keys are. And young Willie ain't likely to try to escape with that shoulder. You must've got him with your Winchester." Dobie glanced at Longarm's rifle resting across one corner of the table.

"Maybe you know more about guns than you think."

"You don't have to be long on the frontier to know the difference between a hole carved by a pistol and one carved by a rifle. The kid said there's two more back where you plunked him."

"I reckon with my aching arm an' all, I forgot to mention them."

"I sent Pedro Estevan and his brother-in-law for 'em. Told 'em to take 'em over to the undertaker, Turnbull." Dobie sniffed and shook his head as he traced circles on the table with his empty schooner. "With all this business, old Everett will think *he's* died and gone to heaven!"

Longarm was staring at the table while thoughtfully smoking his nearly done cheroot. The town marshal waved a hand in front of his face. "There you go again. I sure would like to know what you're thinking, or don't you federal boys think we local ones are smart enough to cipher through it."

Longarm chuckled, blew out his last puff, dropped the cigar on the sawdust-covered earthen floor, and ground it out with his heel. "Matter of fact, I was thinking how you're probably right, Dobie. With all these dumbasses out looking for the stolen loot, most of 'em probably half-drunk and kill-crazy with greed, we might never know who killed who . . . or who in the hell has the loot. Besides, whoever has it might have flown the coop by now, and all these yahoos are running around like dead chickens in vain."

"I doubt he's left," Dobie said. "Anyone leaves a mining camp at a time like this attracts a whole lot of attention. Someone would have mentioned it, and half the camp—or, hell, the *entire* camp!—would have run them down by now."

"You think it's still around then."

Dobie hiked a shoulder and glanced toward the front tent flap as several windburned men sauntered in, looking haggard and edgy in their fur coats and hats, a couple tugging mittens from their stiff hands with their tobacco-stained teeth. Dobie canted his head toward them. "*They* seem to, since they're still here, come back to rest up for another outing tomorrow most likely."

Dobie turned to the men and yelled dryly, "Hey, Landry—how many of you loot chasers swapped lead out there today? I hope you hauled your dead back to Turnbull, or he'll be mighty disappointed."

A beefy, red-cheeked gent in his late twenties scowled at Dobie as he approached the bar. "Aw, hell, Marshal, we ain't loot chasers." He threw a beefy arm over the shoulders of the big man beside him and laughed. "Me and the boys are out scoutin' fresh color!"

Dobie looked at Longarm and chuckled ruefully.

Longarm polished off his beer. "I don't really know why, but I think I'll go up and scout that mine of ole Pete's around Grizzly Ridge. Maybe have a talk with that poor Manduke fella beforehand. At the moment, I have nothing else to scout. You'll draw me another map?"

"The first one keep you from getting lost out there?"

"It would have helped a smarter man."

Dobie chuckled and tapped his schooner. "Another?"

"My turn." Digging in his pocket for change, Longarm shivered. "Damn, it gets cold here of a night!"

Not long after Longarm had bought the second round of surprisingly good ale, adding a shot of busthead for himself and his arm, which had begun throbbing again, more windburned and sunburned men filtered into the tent. Most had obviously been out riding the long coulees, searching for the loot. As they sat talking lazily, fighting the chill that even the big potbelly stove couldn't hold at bay, Longarm and Marshal Dobie were often the targets of guilty glances or, in some cases, threatening sneers.

Longarm was glad he had his rifle resting across the table.

The front flap was thrown back once more, and a man stepped into the tent, looking around suspiciously. The man's eyes floated across the smoky, crowded room, in which Smoke hustled mugs and schooners of his locally famous ale to the yelling, quarreling crowd. Longarm, regarding the newcomer, who wore two old cap-and-ball pistols on his hips, edged a hand toward his Winchester.

The newcomer's eyes held steady on someone a couple tables to the left of Longarm and Dobie, and he strode between the tables and the pine-log stools, trying to look nonchalant by hooking his thumbs behind his cartridge belt and moving slowly. But he continued to swing his head around tensely, as though afraid of being spotted.

He stopped beside the chair of a big, black-haired man who'd thrown his buffalo coat across his chair back. He leaned down to whisper something in the big man's ear, continuing to shuttle his owly gaze around the smoky room suspiciously. His lips moved for about ten seconds. Then he straightened, gave the big man's shoulder a meaningful squeeze, and headed back to the front of the tent and outside.

Longarm followed the man with his eyes, then shuttled his gaze back to the big man, who rose from his

chair, yawning and tossing his poker hand onto the table. Scratching his chest, stretching, and announcing
overly loudly that it was time for bed, he donned his
coat and pushed and shoved his way to the door. His
fellow poker players stared after him, scowling incredulously and muttering amongst themselves.

Dobie caught Longarm's eye. The town marshal was
smiling knowingly as he canted his head toward the
table which the big man had just left. "Watch this," he
yelled to be heard above the din. "This is how it plays
out . . . two, three times a week."

Dobie scrunched down in his chair and folded his
arms across his chest with a look of bemused self satis-
faction.

The men at the big man's table began conversing fer-
vently amongst themselves, their expressions growing
angrier and angrier. Finally, one slammed a fist on the
table, rose, and, shrugging into his blanket coat and
shoving his briar pipe into his pocket, started tripping
over chairs as he headed toward the door. The others at
his table followed, quickly buttoning coats and pulling
fur or wool hats onto their heads.

The other men in the room looked after them, suspicion spreading like a wildfire. Gradually, by ones and
twos, the others rose from their tables or stepped away
from the bar, and stumbled toward the tent's front flap.

"I'll be goddamned," Longarm said to Dobie, surrounded by men stumbling toward the door. "It's a
damn stampede."

"Yup," Dobie said, grinning down low in his chair.
"But I'll bet you ten to one it's based on some crazy
rumor not about a new gold discovery, but about the

stage loot. Someone's seen it or heard from someone who's seen it or seen someone looking mighty suspicious, like they might've found it."

Longarm puffed one of his last two cheroots and swung his head around as nearly the entire room swarmed around him and out the front tent flap, leaving only a few wizened old-timers shaking their heads over their beers. The apron, Smoke, stood near the potbelly stove with three freshly poured schooners on the wooden tray in his beefy hands, bunching his thick lips with anger.

Longarm cocked a brow at Dobie. "Any reason why we should follow along, check it out?"

"Nope," Dobie said with a grin, shaking his head slowly. "If someone did find it, we'll know about it soon enough."

"Figured." Longarm finished his beer, dropped his cigar stub into the mug with a steamy hiss, and rose. "Reckon I'll scratch out a nest somewhere. Any suggestions?"

"Mrs. Meyer's boardinghouse," Dobie said. "West edge of town. The creek'll lull you to sleep." The marshal polished off his beer and rose. "I'll show you. Time I made my rounds anyway. Gotta make sure no drunks are out sleeping where they'll freeze to death. That should be my only trouble for the next day or two . . . till those fools come back and drown their sorrows with drinking and fighting."

"Obliged."

"Don't mention it. I'll ride out to Grizzly Ridge with you tomorrow, if you want."

"You're the town marshal—you best stick close to

the camp. I'll see about Grizzly Ridge. It's probably a long shot, but I'd appreciate that map just the same . . . even if I can't follow it."

"You got it."

The lawmen buttoned their coats and bulled out the tent flap, lowering their heads and squaring their shoulders against the crisp night wind howling with seeming ominous portent through the virtual ghost town of Tin Cup.

Chapter 13

Mrs. Meyer was a chuckling, portly widow—her husband, Oscar, had drowned while panning for gold beneath a beaver dam—with a club foot.

Despite the fact that her face was as wrinkled as fir bark, not a single strand of gray hair shone in the beehive bun atop her head. She fed Longarm a sandwich of bear meat and goat cheese, with a tall glass of cold milk from her own cow, then supplied him with a tin bucket of coal to feed the brazier in his room and showed him upstairs.

As she limped up the staircase, holding a kerosene lantern shoulder high, she glanced back at Longarm and pressed a finger to her lips. "We must be quiet. Poor Silas Manduke came in with a broken arm and went straight to bed. Soggy must have fixed him up good."

She was referring to Manduke's snores resonating loudly, drunkenly, from behind one of the ten or so doors facing both sides of the hall, which was floored in whipsawed pine, as were its walls, without the slightest adornment anywhere.

She'd told the lawman earlier that he was only her second boarder, as all her "boys," as she called them, were off "gallivanting around them darn hills looking for an easy feed like they didn't know no better!"

She left the lantern with Longarm, and limped off down the hall, huffing and puffing and trying to lightly drag the low, hard heel of the shoe on her club foot. The room was only about eight by ten, with a small bed, a washstand, a coat hook, a hide-bottom chair, and a small coal brazier hunkered out of the way in a corner.

It was as much as or more than Longarm had expected in this remotest of remote environs. After building a fire in the stove, he shucked out of his clothes, took two liberal pulls from his bottle of Maryland rye, and burrowed under the sheets, wool blankets, and star quilt.

Before the corn shucks had ceased whispering around beneath him, he was asleep.

He woke later to an icy chill in the room, and noted that the brazier's coals no longer glowed. With a weary groan, clad in his long handles and heavy wool socks, he yawned sleepily, rolled out of bed, clomped over to the brazier, and shoved several small shovel loads of coal through the door, giving them a blow till a red flame licked up around the mounded black chunks.

He closed the tin door, and had just started back to bed when a voice from outside rose above the constant rush of the creeks: "Wait! What're ya—*noooo*!"

There was a thud like something solid smashed against bone.

Longarm glanced at the room's single window. He stumbled over the chair, barking his little toe and cursing, as he made for it, and unhooked the latch. Shoving the window open on its rusty hinges, he peered into the boardinghouse's backyard.

A privy sat beside a buggy shed, a wheelbarrow propped against its side. The privy's door hung open, and Longarm could hear its hinges creaking in the slight, chill night breeze. Something lay on the ground before it. In fact, the door seemed to be catching on one end of the long, oblong object.

"Who's out there?" Longarm rasped, not sure he could be heard above the breeze, the creaking door, and rushing creeks.

He stared at the object on the ground in front of the privy, but couldn't make it out. But from this distance in the dark, it sure as hell looked like a man lying there.

"Damn . . . just when I get a good fire goin'," Longarm growled as he fished around in the dark for his clothes. The weariness in him made him want to ignore the body until morning, but the lawman in him told him to haul ass.

When he'd donned his mackinaw—he wasn't going out there without wearing a coat despite being in a hurry—and grabbed his Winchester, he left his room. The timbers creaked around him, and that was the only sound. Manduke's drunken snores had ceased.

Longarm had seen an outside doorway on the second story. He headed for it now, slipping out into the icy night that braced him like a sharp slap. Testing the none-too-solid-looking steps before giving them his full weight, he dropped down into the boardinghouse's side yard.

Loudly racking a shell into his Winchester's breech, so anyone out here would know he was armed, he held the rifle straight out from his right hip as he made for the privy. As he approached the outhouse, the door's creaking grew louder, as did the tapping of the door against a boot toe that stuck straight up in the air. The owner of the boot lay on his back in front of the door.

Silas Manduke had draped a blanket around his shoulders before heading outside to the outhouse. The blanket lay beneath him now, exposing his skinny chest matted with wiry, gray hair. His broken arm was angled across his belly, held in place by a wide, white strip of bed sheeting. He also wore soiled duck trousers, suspenders hanging slack, and unlaced boots. But what caught Longarm's attention was the man's face.

The crisp starlight glistened in the blood gushing from the man's nose, which lay nearly flat, the tip turned sideways and sort of angled up toward Manduke's half-open right eye. The man's chest lay still. There was no question he was dead, smashed solidly with something unforgiving.

A rock maybe. Possibly a rifle butt or the flat side of a shovel.

Longarm looked around the yard. Whoever'd killed the poor man was obviously gone. There were only the crackling stars and the frigid breeze that pinched Longarm's lungs to the size of raisins and made his nose run.

He was looking north, toward the main part of town, when a shadow dashed between cabins. A horse whinnied, and hooves thudded sharply on the frozen ground.

Longarm's heart quickened. Hefting the rifle across his chest, he started running straight north between cabins, sheds, and woodpiles. He cleaved a gap between two business establishments and ran into the main street. The horseback rider galloped off to his left, fifty yards away and heading away fast.

"Hold it," Longarm shouted.

The rider kept going.

Longarm triggered two quick warning shots at the stars.

"Hold it!"

The horse skidded to a reckless halt and spun, the squat rider silhouetted against the twinkling sky. A man's Spanish-accented voice beseeched, *"Don't shoot me, Señor!"*

Then the horse spun again and continued galloping west, before turning sharply north behind cabins and tents and quickly disappearing, the hoof thuds dwindling. Then there was only the breeze again before running footsteps sounded behind Longarm.

The lawman wheeled to see a man-shaped silhouette drop down from a boardwalk. There was a scrape and a raucous ring of a spur, and the man fell into the street, and rolled.

Chester Dobie's voice said, *"God-fucking-damnit!"* As the man climbed to his feet and, breathing hard, strode quickly toward Longarm, there was the glint of starlight on a gun barrel. "What the hell's going on out here? Drop that rifle!"

"It's me, Dobie—Longarm."

"What the Christ?"

Longarm walked out into the street and dropped to a knee to inspect the fresh tracks stamped into the hardening mud and horse manure. He dropped to a knee and ran a gloved finger around one, the finger lingering over the faint star etched into the mud scored by a rear right hoof.

Dobie stood over him, leaning forward to rub a knee. "What were you shooting at?"

"The man riding this horse—same horse Silas Manduke saw out near Grizzly Ridge . . . unless this star is the blacksmith's calling card."

"Why were you shooting at him?"

"He killed Manduke. Another goddamn privy bushwhacker."

"Where's Silas now?"

"Where I found him."

Dobie turned and walked toward Mrs. Meyer's boardinghouse. Longarm straightened and, setting his jaws against the cold that the murmur of the creeks and the sighing of the pines made colder somehow, stared off in the direction that the horseback rider had galloped.

When he met up with Dobie standing over Silas Manduke, the prospector's blanket buffeting in the wind around his scrawny shoulders and broken arm, the town marshal said, "Flattened his nose. Probably shoved it back into his brain."

"Looks like a gun butt or the back of a miner's shovel."

"A shovel?" Dobie grunted. "That's my calling card."

"I hate to relieve you of your delusions, Marshal, but miners have been killing each other with shovels since the first caveman spied the first color in the first cave wall."

"Yeah, well, Christ—what's going on here?"

"It's too cold for me to think straight, but it appears that the hombre who's been skulking around Grizzly Ridge wanted Manduke out of there. That tells me the man's a claim jumper."

"Maybe that's a good sign," Dobie said. "If these scalawags are back to killing each other for mine claims, then maybe they're starting to give up on the stage loot."

"The rider I tried to stop with my warning shots spoke with a Spanish accent. Any other Mexicans in town besides your odd-job man?"

"Pedro Estevan?" Dobie wrinkled his brows as he stared down at Silas Manduke. "Can't recollect offhand, but I believe there's been a few through here."

Longarm crouched with a sigh over Manduke, folded the flaps of the blanket across the dead man's chest. "You wanna haul him over to the happiest undertaker on the western slope, or leave 'im here and wait till morning?"

"We best haul him over to Turnbull's now." Dobie holstered his pistol, hitched up his pants, and flexed the knee he'd fallen on. "Coyotes might start on him if we leave him here."

Crouching, Longarm and Dobie each grabbed an end of Manduke, and hauled the man over to Turnbull's place. They didn't bother waking the undertaker, but just left the body with several others awaiting burial in the shed behind the man's cabin.

"Not much more we can do tonight," Dobie said, latching the shed's door behind him.

"Nope. Besides, it's too damn cold. I'm liable to wake with my pecker froze to my thigh."

"Don't feel like the lone rider."

"Well, we'll pick up where we left off in the morning," Longarm said.

Then, bidding the marshal good night, he headed for his bed at Mrs. Meyer's boardinghouse.

Longarm jerked his head up from his pillow, and groaned and blinked at the buttery light angling through the window. Christ, it must be damn near ten o'clock in the morning. Last night, he'd asked Mrs. Meyer to wake him at seven. He'd wanted to get an early start for Grizzly Ridge.

The place was twenty miles away through rugged country. If he left right now, without breakfast, he wouldn't arrive at Tin Cup Pete and Silas Manduke's first claim until mid-afternoon. He threw his blankets and star quilt back, and hardened his jaws against the room's sharp bite.

"Wait a minute . . ."

He crawled out of bed, shivering and tucking his cold cock back into his long handles' fly, and tramped over to the window, the toes of his socks flopping out ahead of him. He squinted out the window. There was a pale, crisp coating of frost on the sagebrush and bunchgrass around and between the town's cabins and tent shacks. Smoke lifted from a half dozen chimney pipes. A scrawny red fox with a tail half again as long as its body was sniffing around the privy where Longarm had found Silas Manduke last night.

There was no one else out and about—at least, no one Longarm could see from his second-story window.

"Shit," he said with a chuckle, arching his back with a stretch and running his hands back through his hair, pulling at it brusquely to wake himself up. "It ain't late a'tall. I bet it ain't but seven o'clock if that."

He'd forgotten how early the morning came to the high country, how bright the light could be at the high, dry altitudes in spite of the cold. Up here, it probably froze solid every night through June.

He checked his old Ingersoll watch: 6:37. Good. He'd get an earlier start than he'd figured, arrive at the mine in time to have a look around, and return to Tin Cup before good dark. Just as the morning came early to the high rocks and scraggly pines, night fell late.

He washed and dressed and, with saddlebags and rifle sheath in tow, headed downstairs to surprise the chuckling Mrs. Meyer, toiling at her big, black range, with his early appearance. She fed him a hearty breakfast of eggs, bear meat, and potatoes fried with wild onions and turnip bits, then filled him a lunch sack and, still chuckling, waved good-bye as he tramped off to the livery barn for Duke.

One of the three or four people he spied outside their huts was the undertaker, Turnbull, whistling contentedly as he nailed another pine coffin together outside the open doors of his shed, a wad of nails in his gloved fist and a yellow cur sleeping in the dust at his feet. A body covered with a couple of horse blankets sprawled back-down across a bed constructed of pine boards and saw-horses behind the undertaker. One pale, bony hand hung below the edge of the blankets.

Silas Manduke, no doubt.

Longarm grimaced and nipped the end from his last nickel cigar. He wondered when the bodies were going to stop piling up on this assignment, and something told him, twenty minutes later as he lit out of Tin Cup astraddle Duke for Grizzly Ridge, it wouldn't be anytime soon.

Chapter 14

In spite of the intense, golden sunlight, the cold mountain air required a coat until around ten, and then Longarm stopped by a creek to let the buckskin drink and to wrap his mackinaw around his bedroll. There was still a clear film of ice along the edges of the narrow stream, where the willows stretched their shade, but it cracked like rice paper under Longarm's boot toe, and he topped off his canteen with the frigid snowmelt.

He followed a couple of valleys over two divides that looked out on a devil's playground of snowcapped ridges. Around eleven-thirty, he followed a wagon trail up a steep ridge through firs and aspens, with a beaver meadow appearing now and then through the woods on his right. There must have been rain or snow up here in the last day or so, because the trail was muddy in places, and he didn't see many horse tracks—mostly coyote, raccoon, and fox tracks etched a few hours ago.

But a few times he spied the faint, star-marked shoe print that Silas Manduke had mentioned—the same track as that in the street last night in Tin Cup, behind the man with the Spanish accent who'd fled in the wake of the Manduke killing.

There was a loud, thundering crash up the steep bank on Longarm's left. Heart thudding, the lawman slipped his Colt from his holster and thumbed back the hammer, expecting to see a horse and rider galloping toward him and a gun blasting.

A molting shoulder appeared amongst some stout aspens, and then a broad cream rump flashed as the elk wheeled amongst the trees and fled up the ridge. The thumping of its hooves on the spongy turf dwindled gradually. Longarm raised his Colt's barrel and, his heart slowing, depressed the hammer.

"Gettin' damn jumpy."

He dropped the revolver back into its holster and booted Duke up the steep, meandering trail.

A few minutes later, buildings appeared in the woods on both sides of the trace—a shack and a privy on the left, a hay barn, horse stable, and a peeled log corral on the right. Moss shone green on the brush roofs of the cabin and the barn, and shrubs had grown up around their crumbling stone foundations. There was the musty smell of rotting wood and trash and an old privy hole. A hole low in the cabin's plank-board door had likely been chewed out by a fox or a coyote looking for a den. The place had been abandoned for years. Like Dobie had said, it was a long trek up here, so likely no one else had reclaimed it after Tin Cup Pete and Manduke had pulled out.

Longarm put Duke on up the trail between the cabin and the barn, following a sharp left curve until he was directly above and behind the cabin. Through the woods on his right, the rocky, snow-mantled peak of Grizzy Ridge glowed in the sunshine. In the foreground, only about fifty yards away, was an old mine portal in the side of the slope, surrounded by brush and aspens that had only just started showing some green.

Two log walls lined the side of the hole cut into the slope. Between the walls was a door much like that of the portal at Mirror Lake. The timbered door, showing moss between the heavy pine planks, didn't appear to have a lock on it.

Longarm stepped from his saddle, dropped Duke's reins, and climbed the hill for a closer look. Not only was there no lock on the door, but the door stood a few inches open. Recent boot tracks could be seen in the sand and gravel in front of it.

Cautiously, one hand on his Colt's grips, Longarm wrapped a hand around the side of the door, and drew it back toward him. The rusty hinges made a singsong sound. A cool must from inside the cave wafted against him, and a rat squeaked. There was the scuttle of tiny feet as Longarm, pulling the door as wide as it would go, ducked his head to step inside the cave.

Beyond the door, the ceiling was high enough that, if he removed his hat, he could stand up straight. Beyond the light emanating from the door, he couldn't see much but darkness. He took several steps inside. Someone had been here recently. Maybe only Manduke, working the claim, but it was doubtful the prospector would have left the door unlocked when he'd left.

Longarm's boot caught on something soft and yield-

ing. At almost the same time, he smelled the oily tang of
leather. Dropping to one knee, he reached into the darkness before him and, sure enough, his hand closed over
a leather pouch.

Saddlebags. Both pouches were swollen and hard.

Feeling around in the darkness, he found another set
of saddlebags.

His heart quickened with the thrill of the find. It must
be the same feeling, he thought absently, that drove men
to dig holes and pan streams in remote places long after
good sense told them to leave.

Longarm grabbed both sets of saddlebags, lifting
them. Damn heavy. At least seventy-five pounds each.

Crouching and grunting, he dragged them a few feet
back toward the portal. The midday light fell across
the cracked leather bags, the pouches so swollen that
the flap straps were only barely buckled. Along the
side of one of the gaping flaps, dark green paper could
be seen.

Again, Longarm's heart quickened. His hands tin-
gled.

"What the hell have we here?" he heard himself mut-
ter in a voice he hardly recognized.

An oblong shadow darkened the pouches and just
outside the door, a boot crunched gravel. At the same
time, a man said, his voice startlingly loud in the close
confines, "Roughly a hundred thousand dollars in gold
coins and paper certificates. Enough loot for a man to
live pretty high on the hog for a long damn time."

"Dobie?"

The silhouette wagged the revolver in its hand. "Toss

your gun over here, Longarm. Sorry it had to play out like this. It wasn't how I planned it. But then, Christ, does anything ever go the way you plan it?"

Longarm stared up in shock at the black oval of the marshal's face.

"Come on," Dobie said. "Give me a couple minutes to get used to the idea of killing a federal lawman. If you press me, though, I'll go ahead and do it now." He wagged his gun again. "Toss the hogleg over here, at my feet. Nice and slow. Then that little derringer you wear for a watch fob."

Slowly, Longarm reached across his belly, slipped his Colt from its holster, and tossed it onto the hard-packed dirt floor near Dobie's feet. He considered his chances of springing off his heels and diving at Dobie without getting shot, and decided he'd better wait and come up with another tactic. He pulled the double-barreled, pearl-gripped derringer from his vest pocket, snapped it free of the watch chain, and tossed it down with the .44.

"Got anything else on ya?"

"Folding barlow in my pocket . . . if you consider that something el . . ."

Longarm let his voice trail off as another figure slowly turned from behind the front wall to stand beside Dobie in the open doorway. The sun flashed in her golden blond hair, and her breasts swelled her light pink blouse tucked into a long, green riding skirt secured with a wide, black belt. She also wore a fringed vest with beads in the Ute pattern. A hat hung down her back from a thong around her neck.

Dalia Duchaine rested her elbow on Dobie's shoulder, and smiled, rolling her eyes from the town marshal to Longarm. "Have we defanged the bobcat?"

"As much as we need to, since he's not going to be around much longer."

"Well, I'll be tickled by a horned toad," Longarm said with a caustic laugh. "I am getting too old for this shit!"

Dalia laughed bitterly. "Did you really think my devoted husband would go to all the emotional and physical strain of robbing the stage and then *not* telling me where he hid the money?"

Longarm's cheeks burned as he admitted with no small amount of chagrin, "I reckon you had me believing just that."

"Raise your hands shoulder high and step back," Dobie ordered Longarm, waving his Remington. "A good, long way back."

"When did you move the loot?" Longarm asked.

"A couple days before you got here. Figured the trail would lead you there, so I sent you there myself."

"I just don't understand," Longarm admitted again with open chagrin. "You're the one that called in federal help."

"I told you to raise your hands and step back!" Dobie's voice had a nervous edge. He raised his pistol and rocked back the hammer. The ratcheting click echoed off the portal's rock walls.

"All right." Longarm raised his hands and stepped farther back into the shadows. "I'm goin', I'm goin'."

Dobie glanced at the woman. "Dalia, hold your gun on him. He so much as twitches, shoot him."

Dalia took a deep breath, lifting those full breasts and further swelling her blouse and vest, and slipped her pearl-gripped .36 Smith & Wesson from the holster on her hip. "Don't worry. I'll never see this kind of money again. He moves, I shoot. No questions or warnings."

"You're sweet," Longarm said.

"That's how they make them where I come from."

As Dobie moved forward, watching Longarm as though he was a bear in an inadequate cage, the federal lawman said to Dalia, "Where are you from? I don't reckon we ever got to that, bein' so busy with other matters . . ."

"Shut up!"

Crouching and grabbing both sets of saddlebags, Dobie glanced back at Dalia. "What other matters?"

"Don't listen to him, Ches. He's just trying to rile you. If he doesn't shut up, I'm going to end his feeble attempts at trickery right fast."

Dobie dragged the saddlebags back to the door. Then, straightening and breathing heavily, he said, "I figured calling in a federal lawman would settle everything down. You'd do your investigation, interrogate the mourning widow of Tin Cup Pete, decide she didn't know where the loot was. You'd have a look around and decide the money was nowhere to be found."

"And all the good citizens of Tin Cup would figure I was right?"

Dobie shrugged. "Oh, maybe not right away. But it would speed up the settling down. People hate the government, but secretly they respect it. It'd take the wind out of their sails, anyway."

"And then, after everyone's gone back about their

business, you and the lovely widow lady would slip away in the middle of some chilly damn night with the loot, and by the time anyone got suspicious, you'd be in Mexico."

"Give the man a cigar," Dalia said with a smile.

"Everyone around here knows I wasn't cut out to be a lawman. I'm a failed furniture maker, remember? I only pinned on the badge because Marshal Lewis was desperate for a second man, and the money was better than scooping coins out of slop buckets for whiskey."

"But instead of settling things down," Longarm said, "I only stirred the pot, brought bushwhackers out of the woods like tree fairies. Sort of started a feeding frenzy. All these cork-headed rock breakers decided they wanted to find the loot before I fucked everything up. I reckon that explains Yancy Carruthers and his friend in Hope Creek on my way up here."

"And last night you ran into Silas Manduke." Dobie narrowed a cunning eye. "He'd been up here messing around, even spied my horse tracks. I was afraid he'd found the cache, or was getting suspicious. Looks like he was working a hole farther north, but for all I knew he'd been up here and saw my padlock on the door here."

"And I said I was going to talk to the man." Longarm let his face go slack with regret. "So you killed him before I could talk to him."

"You got it, lawdog."

"You cold-blooded son of a bitch."

"Smashed him with a shovel," Dobie said with a chuckle. "I was afraid I'd miss him if I tried a gunshot in the dark. I've had quite a bit of practice with that shovel over the past year and a half, believe me."

"What about the tracks in the street, behind the Mex?"

As if in response to Longarm's question, a man outside said in a thick Mexican accent, "Señor Dobie, the horses are prepared. All is ready, Señor . . . Señora . . ."

Breathing heavy, a short, squat Mexican climbed the slope behind Dobie and Dalia. He wore a cream sombrero from which untrimmed black hair fell over his ears. A long mustache drooped down around both sides of his wide mouth. The chain of a pocket watch residing in the pocket of his black wool vest winked in the noon sunshine.

"I don't know if you two have been formally introduced," Dobie said with mock seriousness, half turning toward the Mexican moving up behind him and Dalia. "But this is Pedro Estevan. Odd-job man about town. I sent him out on my lightning-fast gelding to fetch Dalia, to tell her to meet me here this morning. Change of plans, and all that." Dobie shook his head warily. "I sure didn't realize my tracks were so conspicuous. I had Pedro remedy that last night when he returned to Tin Cup. Oh . . . and we took a different route from yours up here this morning."

Dobie must have seen Longarm's questioning gaze directed at the Mexican. He said, "Pedro only just learned last night about my and Dalia's little secret. He's agreed to a quite substantial fee—relatively speaking, of course—to help us get the loot out of here and on a train at Gunnison. And to keep quiet."

Dalia snapped a wild look at the town marshal. "Why don't you go ahead and tell him the whole damn plan, Ches?"

"Don't worry, my sweet," Dobie said. "He won't be alive long enough to spoil our plans. Hell, I could tell him about the ship we're going to catch at Monterrey, bound for Honduras."

"Honduras," Longarm said with a whistle. "What the hell are you two going to do down there?"

"The amount of money in those saddlebags," Dalia said with a satisfied arch of her splendid brow, "will go quite far in Honduras . . . all across South America, in fact."

"Better watch her down there, Ches," Longarm said. "A woman with her charms might start casting her wayward eyes around . . . find a charming South of the Border type to help her spend her money . . ."

"I told you to shut up, goddamnit, Custis!"

"Custis?" Dobie snapped an indignant look at his partner in crime. "When the hell did you two end up on a first-name basis?"

Longarm chuckled wryly.

Dalia's mouth pinched. "Don't go getting surly on me, Ches. Do you wanna get out of here or don't you?"

Dobie just stared at her, his eyes uncertain. "So what that fool kid Willie's been yammering about is true . . ."

Longarm cut his hopeful gaze from Dobie to Dalia and back again.

"What the hell are *you* yammering about, Ches?"

"I'm yammering about what the kid witnessed out at your ranch the other night. The two of you . . . on the porch." The corners of the local lawman's mouth rose slightly, knowingly, and he angled his gun toward Dalia. "I should have known I couldn't trust you. Once a whore, always a whore."

Dalia's chest heaved and her eyes hardened. She held her Smith & Wesson straight down by her side. It twitched in her hand, and Longarm could tell she was about to bring it up.

"Drop the gun, Dalia."

"What're you going to do, Ches? That money is mine."

Dobie's voice teemed with menace. "Drop the goddamn gun, Dalia."

"No." A cunning grin twitched at Dalia's ripe mouth. "You can't do it. Shooting a man is hard enough for you, Ches. Shooting a woman you've made love to?" She shook her head slowly. "You couldn't do it."

Longarm wouldn't get another chance. As both conspirators faced one another, he made his move, bounding off his heels and diving toward Dalia.

She was as wily as a damn cat. She must have sensed it coming. She wheeled toward him. Her Smithy's maw yawned at Longarm's gut. He flung himself to one side.

The gun roared. It sounded like a cannon blast in the mine mouth. Longarm bounced off the wall and hit the hard floor on his left shoulder, his wounded arm sending spasms of pain through his every fiber and momentarily paralyzing him. He glanced up to see Dobie and Dalia, silhouetted against the open door, facing one another from two feet away.

The Smithy barked. Dobie grunted sharply as the

bullet creased his right shoulder. An instant later, he smashed his Remington down hard against Dalia's wrist, and the woman's weapon clattered across the floor.

"*No!*" Dalia screamed, bounding toward Dobie, hands in front of her as though to claw at his eyes.

He stepped back, then smashed his left fist across her cheek—a solid smack that resounded off the mine walls. She groaned and hit the floor like a grain sack dropped from a wagon, arms thrown out from her shoulders, one leg curled beneath a hip, her hair a golden, sunlit wash beneath her head.

Dobie swung his gun toward the federal lawman. Longarm, clutching his throbbing left arm and grimacing, braced himself for a bullet. But Dobie didn't shoot. Breathing hard, his face twisted maniacally, he swung his revolver between the groaning Dalia and Longarm and back again.

Dobie glanced over his shoulder at Estevan crouching there, peering into the cave with his hands on his knees, his black eyes fearful. "Pedro, load the saddlebags onto the horses. We're pulling out."

"*Sí! Sí!*"

The Mexican darted forward and, grunting and sighing, dragged both sets of heavy bags out away from the mine portal and into the sunlight. He dragged them down the slope, dust rising behind him, and out of sight.

Dobie picked up Dalia's gun and shoved it behind his cartridge belt. He swallowed and grinned as Dalia, still groaning, lifted her head and pushed up on her elbows. "You two lovebirds have you a real good time in here together, all right?"

With that, he stepped back and grabbed the door handle.

"Ches, wait!" Dalia cried.

The cry was drowned by the thunderous slam of the heavy door.

Chapter 15

In the stygian blackness, relieved by only a thin strip of sunlight showing along the bottom of the closed door, rocks and gravel fell from between the groaning ceiling support beams. Longarm saw a shadow move between him and the door.

"Ches!" Dalia cried. She slammed her fists against the door's stout timbers. "You've got it all wrong! *Listen to me!*"

On the other side of the door there was a muffled chuckle. The silhouettes of two feet shone in the strip of light, and gravel ground beneath Dobie's boots.

"Ches!" Dalia screamed, shriller, desperately slapping her open palms against the door.

The only reply from outside was the raking thump of a locking bar being dropped into the iron brackets across the door. It was followed by the raspy click of a heavy padlock being locked.

"That money is mine, you son of a bitch!" Dalia shouted as Dobie's boots crunched gravel and the wiry brown bush of the mountain slope as he walked away. Slowly, his footsteps dwindled to silence.

A heavy, taunting, impenetrable silence.

The muffled chirps of birds beyond the heavy door seemed to enhance it.

"Chester," Dalia rasped through a sob.

Longarm watched her shadow slide down the door to the floor.

She continued to sniff and cry, occasionally loosing a bitter curse, as Longarm heaved himself to his feet. He could feel his wound bleeding beneath his bandage, but the pain was dulling. It was drowned partly by the sudden desperation of his situation.

Being buried alive was the last way he'd wanted to leave this world. But if that door was as heavy as it looked, and the lock as solid as it had sounded, there was a good chance that's how he'd cash in his chips. Writhing and gasping for the last few morsels of pent-up air . . .

"Get the hell out of the way," he growled at the sobbing woman. He had no more time for her than he did a scrawny mine rat. She'd fucked him, double-crossed him, and likely gotten him killed.

"I said, get the hell out of the way!" he ordered, sliding her aside with his knee.

"Stop it, damn you!" she cried, swiping a fist across his leg.

She scuttled away, sobbing and cursing into her arm, which was draped across a raised knee. Longarm ran his hands across the door, probing here and there, looking for a weak timber. Finding none, he stepped back, turned his right shoulder toward the door, and rammed his weight against it.

The wood creaked only slightly, unmoving. The dry mountain air had preserved the timbers. Damn near turned them to stone. He gave the door another, desperate slam, and heard the heavy padlock rake softly against the locking bar. That was all.

There was no give in the door at all.

He stepped back and sucked in a draft of musty air.

"Do you think you can break through it?" Dalia asked in a desperate, little girl's voice.

"No, I don't think I can break through it," Longarm growled.

"You're a big man," she said hopefully. "Give it another shot!"

"I'd have as much luck trying to throw you through it, which I might do if you don't shut your trap."

Dalia sobbed a little girl sob, sniffling.

"Ah, shut up," Longarm said, resisting the urge to haul back his leg and kick the woman. He couldn't see her in the darkness against the wall to his left, but he could hear her sniveling into her arm with as much rage and frustration as fear.

She'd gone through the entire charade to be locked up in her dead husband's mine by her partner in larcenous murder. She was as guilty of the murder of Marshal Lewis as Dobie was.

"Teach ya to kiss and lie," Longarm grunted as he turned around to face the rear of the cave, digging a lucifer match from his shirt pocket.

"How in the hell are we going to get out of here?" she

asked. The movement of air behind him told him she was pushing to her feet. She cleared her throat, pulling herself together. "Do you think there's a back way out?"

"Doubt it," Longarm said, snapping the match to life on his belt buckle. "But there might be an air vent." As he moved slowly back into the darkness, the flickering match illuminating only small snatches of wall on both sides and just slightly ahead, he said, "How long you and Dobie been in cahoots anyway?"

She was following him so closely that he could feel her body heat and hear her sharp, desperate breaths.

"What the hell does it matter now?"

"Just curious."

They took several more steps, the only sounds the scraping of their heels on the dusty, rocky floor and the tinny drip of water somewhere far back in the cave. She said, "About a month after they hanged Pete for killing the shotgun messenger, I realized I'd need help getting the money out of the Tin Cup country. Men were watching every step I took, camped out in the woods around my ranch. Dobie knew I knew where the money was—at least he had a strong hunch—and he offered to help . . . for half."

"So you threw in together . . . in more ways than one."

"Oh, Christ," she said sharply, annoyed. "A woman has needs just like a man does."

"The other night, were you fulfilling those needs or trying to shake me from your trail?"

"What do you think?"

"Likely both," he said.

There was a slight wry note in her tone as she responded. He could feel her fingers clinging to the back of his coat as he lit another match and continued walking slowly into the musty cave. "I'm a practical woman, Custis."

"But not all that devoted to Dobie apparently. Nor your recently deceased husband."

"Are you trying to tell me you didn't have a good time?"

"Oh, I had a good time, all right," Longarm growled, lifting his third match toward the ceiling where a cobwebbed ceiling beam hung low. "And now I feel like a damn fool."

She stumbled slightly behind him, and grabbed his coat more firmly to keep from falling. "If it makes you feel any better, you're not the first man I've made a fool of."

"Sorta figured that."

Longarm was thinking that Tin Cup Pete was the biggest fool of all—though likely a happy fool—when she sucked a sharp breath on the heels of a ratcheting screech from somewhere just ahead and above. "Jesus Christ—a fucking rat!"

Longarm had stopped, his ears ringing from the high-pitched squeak, and lifted the match again. Two little round eyes flashed redly. Then the rat wheeled along the ledge it clung to, flicked its whiplike tail, and scuttled off along the ledge and into the darkness.

"I hate those damn things," Dalia rasped.

Longarm continued forward. He expanded his chest with a deep breath, feeling a coolness against his face. Was that fresh air he was breathing, slightly displacing the mustiness and the smell of rat shit and bat guano?

He continued forward, the pinging of the dripping water growing louder ahead of him. The match smoldered down to his fingers, and he hissed against the burn and dropped it. In the heavy blackness of the cave, a faint illumination appeared. It seemed to be the reflection of outside light off the rock wall ahead about thirty yards.

He struck a match, held it out before him, and stopped suddenly, frowning down at his feet.

"Look!" Dalia said, brushing around him and pointing straight ahead. *"Light!"*

"Hold on!"

Longarm lunged forward and grabbed for her arm. Too late. His heart leaped into his throat as the sickening sound of timbers crumbling away beneath his and her feet reached his ears.

Dalia screamed.

Having one foot on solid ground, Longarm tried throwing himself back away from the pit. At the same time, Dalia swung around as she plunged through the breaking, rotten planks, and clawed at him desperately, hooking one hand behind his cartridge belt and trying to pull herself toward him.

It didn't work. She only pulled *him* off the solid ledge toward *her.*

"Sheeeee-itttttt!" Longarm heard himself shout amidst Dalia's echoing scream as together they plunged straight down, broken wood tumbling around their heads and shoulders.

Longarm felt a rock bounce off the side of his head a half second before he saw, growing beneath him, an oily, faintly glistening pool of black liquid. Another half second after that, his boots and Dalia's broke the surface of the black pool and plunged down, down, suddenly weightless and falling slightly backward, their feet rising before them.

Longarm threw his arms out to break his plunge as the murky, frigid water closed around him, pinching the air from his lungs and making his ears ring several octaves higher than Dalia's scream. When he'd hit the water, he'd had his mouth open, and a gallon or so of the cold, foul-tasting liquid shot down his throat and into his belly, instantly setting his gut aflame with cold, nauseating fire.

It was like swallowing a fifty-pound ingot of frozen cow shit.

The pit wasn't deep. When the bottom brushed his boots, he planted his heels and thrust upward, clawing at the water with his hands and arms. His head sprang back above the surface seconds later, and he shook water from his hair and eyes and spat it from his mouth, feeling it coming up from his gut and shooting out his nose.

He gagged, retched, gagged again.

Dalia's besotted head swam into view before him, her face crumpled with shock and misery, mouth open as she screamed, *"Raaats!"*

There was an echoing, indignant peep, and then Longarm saw the rat perched on Dalia's head, looking down as though wondering what in the hell it was sitting on. More movement attracted his attention behind her, and every muscle and sinew in his body contracted.

At least a dozen more rats were scrambling along the

narrow rock ledges lining the pit. Not only behind Dalia, but behind him, too . . . and *all around them!*

"Jumpin' Jesus!" Longarm grunted and, lunging toward Dalia, cuffed the rat from her head.

The furry rodent hit the water with a muffled screech, righted itself, and began furiously swimming for the ledge ten feet away. Treading water, hearing Dalia groaning, "Oh, God! Oh, God!" Longarm looked around and up.

The pit was about ten feet deep and about that wide across. Ledges had been chipped out of the walls surrounding it—likely by Tin Cup Pete and Silas Manduke as they followed a vein straight down—and the cracked, chipped shelves should give a good enough purchase for climbing the hell out of here.

"Grab the side!" Longarm shouted, his voice echoing crisply in the stone-walled pit. He grabbed Dalia's arm and shoved her toward the same side of the pit that the rat had been heading toward.

"No! God, can't you see them?"

"You wanna stay here and drown?"

As he reached for a small, bricklike ledge at the side of the pit, the squeaking rats scurried away from him like cockroaches from a lantern. "They're just rats!" he shouted as much to himself as to her, suppressing a shudder. "They're not grizzly bears. The most they can do is give ya a little nip!"

"Oh, Jesus!" the woman wailed. She clung to a rock thumb near Longarm, facing him, her breasts heaving above the surface of the churning water, the nipples sharply jutting from the chill. "I'd rather fight a grizzly! *I hate rats!*"

"Don't tempt me to leave you here, missy—that'd be too damn easy!" Longarm grabbed her other hand and swung her around to face the wall. "Come on—we're gonna climb the hell outta here."

He grabbed his soaking hat, mashed it down on his head, then ground his right boot heel against the ledge below the water's surface. He pushed himself up while flinging his left hand above his head, latching onto another ledge two feet above the last. He glanced below to see Dalia doing the same as she cast anxious looks at the rats scurrying to and fro around her, berating her and Longarm while flicking their tails angrily, incensed by the intrusion.

If they weren't both in such a sorry predicament, he would have chuckled at hers. She'd thought Longarm would be dead by now, and she and Chester Dobie would be hauling their loot out of the mountains toward Gunnison. Singing along with the songbirds and planning how they were going to spend all that loot, maybe giving each other optimistic pecks on their smiling cheeks and chuckling at her husband's stupidity.

Not to mention Longarm's.

"Oh, *Gawd!*" she cried as a rat made an angry dash for her, as though to chase her off the ledge before wheeling and squealing and flicking its tail off into the shadows.

Longarm, who'd climbed halfway out of the pit, his soaked clothes dripping into the water below, reached down and grabbed her wrist. She groaned painfully and looked up at him in horror as he muscled her up beside him and held her there as her flailing feet searched for a

ledge. When she found one, Longarm bunched his lips
and began hauling her farther up the pit.

"*Ow,* you *bastard*!" she bellowed. "You're hurting
my *wrist.*"

"Get a move on, goddamnit!" he bellowed back with
a savage grunt, hauling her up above him, then shoving
her up by placing the heel of his hand on her round,
firm, wet ass. "I don't wanna spend all day down here
listening to you lecture the damn rats!"

He kept pushing her up the ledge as he climbed,
groaning at the sting in his left arm and feeling blood
mixing with the water inside his shirtsleeve. The pain
made him all the angrier and all the more eager to get
the hell out of the mine shaft, and he kept pushing Dalia
savagely up the pit wall until she'd finally disappeared
up and over the edge. She gave a cry of relief and scuttled away from the ledge, back into the shadows, as
Longarm hauled his own weary self over the top.

He lay back down on the cave floor, hanging his legs
over the pit's edge and breathing heavily, occasionally
choking on the sour water still working its way up from
his lungs.

After a time, he rolled over and gained his feet heavily. She sat back against the wall, elbows resting on her
raised knees, head down, wet hair hanging down both
sides of her face. Faintly, the light from ahead shone on
her wet skin and clothes.

"Come on." He pulled her up by her arm. "No time
to dally."

She groaned, but seemed too tired to fight him. When
he had her standing, he started forward again, watching
the floor carefully for more flooded pits covered with

rotten planks, and made his way toward the wan light reflecting off the chipped, pocked left wall of the cave.

Silently, he begged forgiveness for his misspent years, and prayed that the light would show him a way up and out of this hell.

Chapter 16

Longarm placed his hand on the woman's wet bottom and pushed.

"Goddamnit, will you please take your hand off my ass?"

"That ain't what you said the other night."

Dalia Duchaine told Longarm to do something physically impossible to himself.

"Not until we're out of here," the lawman said, his voice echoing off the narrow walls of what he had indeed found to be an air vent.

The vent was about three feet square, one hell of a tight fit, and if he got stuck, he didn't want Dalia behind him. So he'd made her go first, climbing the slightly angling tunnel toward the blue patch of sky hovering above. The trouble was, the place was coated with bat guano, and occasionally a bat would screech and whip its wings around the top of the vent, and she'd stop to curse and shudder.

Longarm pushed her up with the heel of his hand and, having little choice, the woman began climbing again, digging her boots into the fissures and crevices lining the chimney. "I believe you're enjoying this."

"Not a bit, lady," Longarm said, wincing as he wiggled his shoulders through a tight spot and pushed up with his heels. "I'm not gonna enjoy one damn thing ever again until I've hunted down that son of a bitch partner of yours and his Mex sidekick and throwed all three of your sorry asses in the hoosegow and dropped the key down the privy hole!"

She groaned and climbed, and the light grew gradually stronger as Longarm came up behind her, giving her a push when she slowed. His breathing was tight and it grew tighter when the uneven walls of the chimney closed taut about his shoulders, threatening to pin him there. Longarm didn't like rats or bats, and he sure wasn't enjoying the proposition of dying in there, trapped in a tunnel with rats beneath him and bats above.

A rock grazed his temple and bounced off his shoulder before continuing to clatter down the chimney below him. Pain bit him, and he looked up, grinding his molars in anger.

Dalia looked down, a smile shaping her mouth. "Oh, sorry."

"Fuckin' bitch." Longarm set his hand on her bottom and pushed.

She gave a squeal and continued climbing.

After what seemed like a month, but was probably only another fifteen minutes, Longarm pushed the woman up and out of the top of the chimney. He followed, nearly finding himself trapped at the lip, where the vent wall had bulged inward. He knew a terrifying moment before, with a bearlike growl of rage, he ripped a chunk of rock out from the bulge with his fist and let it drop back into the mine shaft below.

He heaved his shoulders up out of the vent, and hoisted himself with a gargantuan effort out of the hole that seemed to suck at him like the mouth of a giant snake. With a sigh, he sprawled on the sloping, needle-matted ground, and drew great draughts of air into his lungs as he stared at the sky through gnarled pine crowns. He felt a smile lift the corners of his mustached mouth, and giddiness tempered with disbelief danced through his head.

Had they made it, or was he dreaming as he slowly drowned in the rat pit?

Dalia appeared between him and the sky. Staring down at him, her jaws hard, eyes narrowed, she held a large rock straight up above her head. Longarm whipped his left leg out and back, scissoring her feet out from beneath her. She screamed as she fell and smashed her back against the ground, the rock tumbling down the slope behind her.

She gave a great *whoosh!* as the air left her lungs in one, sudden rush.

"Bastard!"

Longarm rolled onto a hip and shoulder, chuckling. "You sure are mouthy for a good Catholic girl."

She bit her lip with pain and pushed up on her elbows. She shot him a savage look and opened her mouth, but before she could speak Longarm said, "Yeah, I know. 'Go fuck yourself.'"

He got up heavily, his clothes wet and muddy and spotted with bat guano and rat shit, and looked around.

The pines up there on the shoulder of the mountain were tall and spindly. Looking through them, he saw the mine shack and the barn down the slope and to the right. Beyond the buildings lay a beaver meadow, the clear pools and the low, white falls flashing like sequins in the sunshine.

"Reckon I'll get cleaned up and look for my hoss," he grunted, and started walking, floppy-footed with exhaustion, down the slope through the firs and pines.

He wasn't worried about Dalia running off. Without a horse, there was nowhere for her to go. She'd be stranded out there with no food, only water. And she knew the country well enough to know you didn't want to be stranded out there, twenty miles from town, without food and weapons.

He was so fatigued from his ordeal in the mine that he nearly fell several times as he made his way down the slope past the barred door of the mine portal, past the cabin and the barn and farther down the slope to the meadow. He didn't bother looking around for Dobie's tracks. He'd find them later, and he'd shadow the man until he'd run him to ground.

If Dobie hadn't taken Duke, that is . . .

The concern vanished as Longarm started across the meadow to a broad pond. A whinny sounded to his left, and he turned to see the buckskin standing at the edge of the meadow, a hundred yards away, reins dangling. Longarm's saddle and rifle boot hung down the horse's side. The Winchester appeared to be in the boot. Longarm grinned. He'd had a feeling the horse would have spooked at Dalia's gunfire inside the mine mouth, and lit a shuck out of there.

Footsteps sounded in the woods behind him, and he turned to see Dalia moving down the slope through the trees, like a walking corpse.

Longarm stumbled forward through the chokecherry scrub and hard clumps of fescue. He pushed through the willows lining the pond, then stepped off the low bank and into the sandy-bottomed pool, the water gurgling and splashing around his legs. Throwing his arms straight out from his shoulders, he sagged straight back and collapsed butt down, letting the pure, sun-warmed water close over him. He pulled his head under and felt his hat rise up from his head and bounce away on the ripples.

He took a long drink, then lifted his head above the surface, sitting up with his legs lolling before him. He reached up and jerked his string tie off, tossed it into the water, and followed it with his shirt. Kicking out of his boots, he wriggled out of his whipcord trousers and cast them aside to be cleaned in the pure snowmelt that caressed his grimy skin like liquid silk. He pushed up off the scalloped sand bottom flecked with small stones and shiny bits of pyrite, and quickly shucked out of his long handles.

He tossed the underwear aside, where it bobbed, turned, and sank, and turned to see Dalia wading into the pond nearby, shucking out of her own clothes and shaking her head so that her drying, muddy hair danced about her shoulders. She saw him looking at her, and she stopped twenty yards away and shucked out of her blouse, throwing her shoulders back so that her jostling breasts stood out proudly. Still staring at him, a bemused smile quirking her lips, she lifted her thin camisole up

and over her head and held it to one side for a time, her
firm orbs fully revealed, then opened her fingers and let
the garment tumble into the water.

"What are you looking at?" she said coyly.

Longarm cleared his throat, which had suddenly become thick and heavy. "A bitch on high red wheels—
that's what."

He forced himself to turn his head away from the
beautiful woman—even beautiful with her hair dirty and
covered in rat and bat shit—and grabbed a handful of
sand from the bottom of the stream. He used the sand to
scrub his arms and his chest. Still keeping his eyes off
Dalia, he stood, ignoring his cock standing at half-mast,
and grabbed up more sand to scrub his thighs and
calves, feet and buttocks.

He could hear her splashing around in the water, doing the same, but he resisted the temptation to look at
her. Her eyes were on him, though. He could feel the
heat of them burning into his cock, making it stand up
straighter and prouder, and he sat down to cover his lust.
He lay straight back in the water, drawing his head beneath the surface, to wash the sand from his body including his head and his hair. He turned, thrashing like a
bathing bear and blowing water out his mouth and nostrils, trying to rid himself of the stench that seemed to
have seeped into his lungs.

When he was done, he stood, water running off his
body, pouring down his face from his hair. He blew it out
of his mouth once more, shook his head, and started
wading toward shore. He'd sit in the grass and dry in the
sun while his clothes soaked in the pond. Opening his
eyes and shaking his hair away from his face, he stopped.

Dalia lolled in the shallows straight ahead of him, only a few feet away. Glistening wet and naked, she leaned back, her arms draped across a bleached log at the edge of the grassy shore. Chin down, her brown eyes smoky, she opened and closed her legs slowly in the clear water, giving him an enticing view of her gold-furred pussy snugged between thighs made muscular from years of outdoor work and horseback riding.

"Want me to take care of that for you?"

Longarm looked down at his throbbing cock, the head like a giant, purple mushroom.

"I'd rather do it myself."

"Oh, come on. No strings attached. We got on rather well the other night." She kicked her foot, splashing him, and canted her head back and to one side. "Don't tell me you haven't thought about it . . . and gotten a hard-on thinking about it. I have . . . and I don't even have a cock."

Her pink-tipped breasts were swollen as they bobbed half out of the water, spilling over the sides of her ribs. Longarm could tell by the look on her face that it wasn't only the cool water making her nipples jut.

Try as he might, Longarm couldn't make himself walk away.

She smiled, rose to her knees, and narrowing her eyes at his throbbing member, crawled over to him and took the shaft in her hand. Caressing it gently, she sat back on her heels and squinted up at him, smiling that inscrutable, coquettish smile.

"Well, then," she said, clearing her throat and smacking her lips. She stroked him harder, bringing the skin up over the head and back down again, caressing his balls with her other hand. "We can't have you going around like this now, can we?"

With that, she leaned forward and closed her mouth over the head of his member. She sucked the tip for a time, then, groaning and turning her head first to one side, then the other, and closing her eyes, slid her lips nearly all the way down to his crotch. Her mouth opened slightly when the tip of his cock slid down her throat, gagging her.

She slid her lips back up again, then down, then up once more, building a quickening rhythm that made the big lawman's heart flutter and his knees so weak, he thought for a time he'd faint.

Afterward, when she'd sucked him dry and swallowed every drop, she sat back on her heels once more and ran the back of her wrist across her lips. She looked up at him, her coy smile in place. "Now, what do you say you and I hunt Dobie down, take all that loot for ourselves? We could have one hell of a fine old time down in South America, Custis."

She leaned forward, dropped her head, and turned her lips upward to nuzzle his balls.

"That's a tempting offer, Dalia. But I'll have to turn ya down. You and Dobie are goin' to jail." Longarm stepped around her and climbed up onto the grass. "I do appreciate the blow job, though. If I didn't know better, I'd say you'd given a few of those before."

He ducked a rock whistling toward his head.

Chapter 17

Blue smoke skeined from the chimney pipe of the squat log cabin, and curled upward toward bowed fir branches softly burnished with the copper of the fading light.

The canyon walls were steep here—two-thousand-foot craggy precipices towering over the Taylor River that made a steady chugging rush right of the cabin. The cliffs cast an ever-deepening blue shadow over the cabin, the woods, and the river itself as well as over the two men tending the leaping, crackling fire between the cabin and the river.

Longarm, crouched over a fallen tree bole fifty yards from the cabin, adjusted the focus on his field glasses. He was close enough that he could hear the men's voices above the river, but he couldn't make out what they were saying.

In the two spheres of magnified vision, the men came into view amidst the columnar pines—the stocky Mexican, yammering and laughing as he hauled firewood up from the river, and Chester Dobie, kneeling in front of the fire and chopping up two dead jackrabbits on the flat

side of a split log. He, too, was chuckling—probably
over how he and Pedro Estevan were going to spend the
loot—as he tossed chunks of meat into the tin pot he'd
set on a rock beside the leaping flames.

A rifle leaned against a log near Dobie. The marshal
wore his own Remington in his holster, and Longarm's
double-action Colt bristled behind the man's cartridge
belt over his belly. Shifting the glasses back to Estevan,
who dumped his wood on the ground beside the spark-
ing fire, Longarm saw that the Mexican wore one pistol
low on his thigh, and he had a Spencer repeater leaning
on a log on the other side of the fire from Dobie.

Damn well armed, both of them.

Farther back in the woods, three hobbled horses
milled, swishing their tails and grazing.

Longarm looked around for the saddlebags stuffed
with the stage loot, but they were nowhere in sight. The
men had probably stashed them in the cabin.

Estevan rocked back on his heels and threw his arms
out to his sides as he held jubilantly forth on something
Longarm couldn't hear while Dobie continued chopping
meat, chuckling, and shaking his head slowly in amused
agreement.

Longarm tightened his jaws and lowered the glasses.

The two were as happy as a couple of drunk whores
at a free-hooch hoedown.

Not for too damn much longer . . .

Growling to himself, the lawman dropped the field
glasses against his chest, where they hung from his neck
by a leather thong, and picked up his Winchester.
Crouching, he backed away from the log, putting several
firs in front of him before wheeling and striding back

toward the clearing along the river in which he'd left Duke and Dalia.

"Did you see them?" the woman asked.

She sat back against a boulder beside the foaming, hammering river, her hands tied behind her back, her ankles tied together in front of her. She'd spat out the wadded neckerchief he'd used as a gag.

"It's them, all right." Longarm ran a calming hand along the buckskin's neck, and dropped his field glasses in his saddlebags. He glanced at Dalia staring at him expectantly, and shuttled the glance to the neckerchief at her feet. "Slipped your bit, did ya?"

"You think I want Dobie making off with my loot?" she snapped. "I'm not going to warn him."

"No, you're not."

Longarm made sure his Winchester was loaded, then grabbed a box of shells from his saddlebags. He stuffed the box into his coat pocket, walked over to Dalia, and picked up the neckerchief. He set his rifle aside, smoothed out the neckerchief, taking both ends between his fingers, and quickly brought the ends around to the back of her head, making sure the front slipped between her delicious lips. She jerked her head from side to side and spat, but Longarm held the neckerchief taut as he double-knotted it behind her head.

"And I don't trust you as far as I could throw you against a Dakota cyclone."

She grumbled and groaned furiously, turning her head from side to side, futilely trying to spit free of the gag.

Longarm picked up his rifle, patted Duke's rump, and strode on past the horse, heading into the woods far left of where he'd gone before. Since Dobie would be expecting trouble from upstream instead of down, and since there was a chance Duke might whinny and give Longarm away, he traced a broad circle around the cabin, keeping to the inky shadows at the edge of the woods.

When he'd curved back around to the river, he hunkered down behind a boulder at the edge of the drumming stream, feeling the icy spray against his cheeks, and stared back upstream. Barely, he could see the fire flickering amongst the pines and aspens, sixty or seventy yards away.

As he started out from behind the boulder, a gunshot sounded.

Longarm dropped to a knee and stared straight ahead toward the cabin. The sound—a little louder above the river's roar than the snapping of a branch across a knee—had come from that direction.

Another pop sounded amidst the river's roar.

Suddenly, the birds and squirrels fell silent, and there was only the scratching of the breeze-brushed branches and the river's incessant churning.

Longarm absently scratched his cheek with a gloved hand as he stared through the trees. Had Dobie discovered Dalia? If so, he'd be on the lookout for Longarm.

The lawman held his position for a time, watching and listening, as more and more light retreated up the walls of the canyon. When a squirrel began chittering again from a nearby branch, he rose and began striding slowly upstream, only a few feet from the river, crouching and holding his Winchester in both hands straight out in front of him.

Slowly, he drew closer to the fire, the smoke slithering up through the branches. In the corner of his eye, something moved on the river. A log.

No. Not a log.

Christ, a man . . .

Longarm stepped to the edge of the stream as the body tumbled between two boulders, twisting and turning in the savage current, and shot toward him down a narrow chute. The Mexican floated on his back, arms and legs jostling this way and that, head jerking, longish hair floating out around his shoulders, as the boiling water pushed and tore at his stocky frame.

He angled toward Longarm as though he were aiming himself in that direction, then arced back out into the stream before getting hung up on a pine that had recently fallen into the river. He floated there, pitching with the fickle current, his denim jacket caught on one of the pine branches.

Longarm twitched with a start as Pedro Estevan's head turned toward him and his lips and jaws moved. The lawman had assumed the Mexican was dead, fed two pills he hadn't been able to digest when Dobie had decided he'd had all the help he needed.

"Por favor," the man said weakly, his voice nearly drowned by the current. He held out his arm, extending his hand. "Help me!"

Longarm took his rifle in his right hand and placed one foot in the river. He'd started extending his left hand toward the Mexican, when the man's jacket tore suddenly. With a barely audible shriek, Estevan was unceremoniously swept under the tree, twirled viciously, and shot back into the stream where he pinwheeled down a low falls and out of sight.

Longarm lifted his boot from the frigid stream, cursing. Now he'd have to be extra careful; the wet boot would squawk when he walked on it.

Quickly, he leaned against the uprooted ball of the fallen tree, removed the boot, poured out the water, and wrung as much as he could from his sock. When he'd donned the boot once more, he continued forward, angling slowly away from the river toward the cabin, meandering around the darkening pines.

Smoke from the fire touched his nostrils, as did the aroma of rabbit stew. As he continued toward the fire, he could hear the flames crackling and snapping, and could see, to his pleasure, Dobie sitting facing the flames with his back toward the stream as the smoke from the fire wafted toward the cabin and into the woods beyond.

Longarm edged a look from behind a tree about twenty yards behind Dobie. The crooked Tin Cup marshal sat on a rock, the saddlebags piled to one side, a Spencer repeater leaning against the pile. A bourbon bottle sat on the ground to the other side, a tin cup beside it. One of the saddlebag pouches was open, spilling clumps of greenbacks bound with brown paper bands. The man's chin was dipped toward his chest, and his arms and hands were moving.

He was counting the cash.

Longarm winced as he stepped forward on his soggy foot. He gently put his weight on it, and winced again as a faint chirp rose from the wet leather.

He looked at Dobie. The man continued busily counting the cash, shuffling the money from one hand to the other.

Longarm took another step. He stopped when Dobie leaned down suddenly, set the wad of greenbacks he'd been counting beside the saddlebags, and grabbed another wad from the open pouch. With a grunt, Dobie straightened in his chair and, waving away a vagrant smoke tendril with one hand, dropped his head and started counting his current greenback wad.

Longarm stopped and leveled his Winchester at Dobie's back, loudly racking a shell into the breech. "However much it is, it ain't enough, you sonofabitch!"

Dobie leaped up off the rock with a startled grunt and, spilling the money onto the ground between him and the fire and kicking over his bourbon bottle, placed his hand on his Remington's grips. Longarm didn't say anything. He just leveled his Winchester at Dobie's belly and smiled savagely.

Dobie kept his hand on the Remy's grips, but left the gun in its holster. He stared at Longarm, his wide eyes betraying the impulses whipping around in his brain.

"Go ahead." Longarm glanced at the Remington. "Pull it. I'd like nothin' better than to gut-shoot you and watch you take a long time to die while I eat your stew."

Dobie shuttled his glance between the rifle aimed at his gut and Longarm's narrowed eyes. His body seemed to deflate at once, shoulders slumping, his hand sliding away from the holstered six-shooter. He lifted his head but kept his shoulders down, and his face slackened with grim defeat.

"How did you get out of the mine?" he said softly.

"If you'd spent any time rock farming, you'd know those things usually have a vent."

Longarm mashed his Winchester's barrel against

Dobie's soft, flat belly. He reached forward, pulled the Remington from its holster, and tossed it away in the brush. Then he grabbed his .44 from behind Dobie's waistband, and dropped it into his own cross-draw holster.

Keeping the Winchester pressed firmly against the town marshal's belly button, he held out his hand. "My derringer."

Dobie sucked a breath and reached inside his black and green mackinaw.

"Slow as chilled honey," Longarm warned, cocking a brow.

Slowly, Dobie pulled the gun out of his shirt pocket. He opened his hand to reveal the double-barreled, pearl-gripped popper resting in his palm.

Longarm took the little gun, shoved it into his coat pocket, and stepped back. He wagged his rifle. "Come on out here, away from the fire, and give me your back, hands behind your head."

Dobie had just started to comply when a rifle barked in the woods upstream from the cabin.

"*Ohh!*" Dobie cried, crouching and grabbing the side of his right thigh.

Longarm jerked back, looking around wildly and bringing his Winchester to bear on the woods.

A second shot blew up dust and sage in front of him, between him and Dobie.

Someone loudly racked a fresh shell in a rifle's breech, and Dalia Duchaine rose from behind a log at the edge of the clearing, aiming an old Colt's revolving rifle at Longarm and Dobie.

The town marshal grunted and cursed as he staggered

miserably, clapping both hands over his thigh from which dark red blood gushed to dribble down his denim pants leg.

Three bearded, fur-clad men bounded up from cover in the woods flanking Dalia, and, leaping fallen logs and shrubs, came whooping and hollering into the clearing like wolves on the blood scent.

Striding calmly but purposefully into the clearing, her Colt rifle aimed straight out from her side, Dalia smiled. "How-do, gents," she said in a lousy Southern accent. "We heared this was where the shindig was at!"

Chapter 18

"I got you dead to rights, Custis," Dalia said as she moved toward him, holding the Colt on Longarm's chest. "You best toss that saddle gun aside or I'll do you the way I did the good marshal of Tin Cup." Her brown eyes flashed toward Dobie. "Jesus, Ches, that has to hurt like *hell*!"

She laughed with glee.

Crouched forward and clutching his leg, Dobie gave a strangled cry and plopped down on his butt.

Dalia held her rifle on Longarm, who cursed, depressed his Winchester's hammer, and tossed the carbine into the brush. The three men—two short and scrawny, the other a big mule of a man with a thick, cinnamon beard—moved up to the fire, snuffling and chuckling and ogling the money pouches like coyotes descending on a sickly elk calf.

"Friends of yours?" Longarm said, rolling his eyes toward the others.

"Only recently," Dalia said. She cut her gaze sharply toward the big man who was striding around Longarm to get at the saddlebags. "Heel, Jeff! We'll go through those bags together."

When the big man, muttering with frustration, had backed away, holding his old trapdoor Springfield on Longarm and cutting his eyes nervously at the money, Dalia glanced at the lawman. "Seems they were trailing us. Suspicious devils. They'd trail a fox if they thought it led to the stage loot."

"So that's it?" said one of the scrawny loot seekers through a snaggle-toothed grin. He stood over Dobie, holding his own Springfield low and negligently angled toward the town marshal's bowed head. "That's it there in them saddlebags?"

"You sure threw in with 'em fast," Longarm commented to Dalia. "How's that deal gonna work?"

Sidling up to Jeff and tossing her hips coquettishly, she reached up to wrap her arm around the big man's neck, pull his head down, and give him a feigned-hungry kiss on his furred lips. Releasing him, she glanced at Longarm with a toxic mix of cunning and deviltry smoldering in her evil brown eyes. "How do you think it's gonna work? These boys have never seen the likes of me . . . and that much money."

"You all gonna go on down to South America together?" Longarm said with mockery. "Have you a high-stepping time down there, are ya?"

He knew that if her three new friends didn't kill her first—after having one hell of a time between her legs, of course—she'd kill them. Back-shoot them the first chance she got. He doubted the three scraggly loot seekers realized it, however. They were drunk with lust and greed.

"Why not?" Dalia said, throwing a well-curved hip out and planting a gloved fist on it. "Jeff, Hyatt, and William here deserve a good time after all the trouble they've had. All the months of searching for the stage loot. They deserve some tender, lovin' care, too, from a good-lovin' woman."

"They'll get that in spades," Dobie croaked out, sitting on his butt and trying to squeeze closed the gushing wound in his thigh.

"Shut up, you son of a bitch, or I'll drill one into your other leg and watch you die slow!"

"Let's go ahead and kill 'em now," Jeff said. "No point in palaverin'. I wanna get at them money sacks." He turned a smoldering smile on Dalia. "And that other we agreed on . . ."

"Good point, Jeff," Dalia said. "You're smarter than you look." She canted her head toward the rushing stream that, in the falling darkness, was a silver glow through the trees. "All three of you, take them down to the river, shoot them, and throw them in. Then come on back and we'll start divvying up those greenbacks!"

"No!" Dobie raked out, diving for the Spencer that Pedro Estevan had left leaning against the log.

Dobie and the snaggle-toothed hard case fired their rifles at nearly the same time. Longarm heard Dobie groan as he, Longarm, reached down and lifted a burning branch from the dwindling fire. He smashed the flaming branch into Jeff's face. Jeff screamed and stumbled back, shaking his head and swiping at the flames with his hands.

Longarm heard the sickening rasps of Dalia and the snaggle-toothed man racking fresh shells into their rifle

breeches as he took a running dive for his Winchester.
The third man hammered a rifle round into the ground
just right of Longarm's right shoulder.

Longarm grabbed the Winchester and bounded off
his heels, moving faster than he'd ever moved before,
sensing three separate targets being drawn on his back,
and dashed behind a tree.

Three racketing shots blasted as Dalia screamed,
"Get him!"

The three bullets tore into the tree on the other side of
Longarm, flinging bark in all directions. As the shooters
levered fresh shells, Longarm bounded forward, dashing
and crouching into the woods, careening around trees.

Dalia and her three new friends hammered lead into
the woods around him. Bullets slammed into tree boles
and branches and blew up puffs of dust and pine nee-
dles. Longarm continued running, tracing a zigzag pattern around the pines and low shrubs, leaping branches
and deadfalls.

He could tell by the yelling and the errant shooting
that they'd lost him.

He stopped, pressed his back against a broad, light-
ning-topped pine, and turned his head to listen. Foot
thuds rose. Dalia was grumbling orders. Occasionally,
one of the three popped off an exploratory shot.

He doffed his hat and edged a look around the pine,
catching a glimpse of Dalia and one of the other men
moving through the trees about forty yards behind and
between Longarm and the stream. From the crunching
footsteps, he could tell the other two men were somewhere off his other flank. They were closer than Dalia
and the other man, and they were edging closer.

Longarm dropped to a knee, twisted around to face away from the river, and waited, tightening his finger against the Winchester's curved trigger.

The crunching footsteps grew louder.

Then one pair stopped.

"He's over here, Hyatt—I can *smell* him," someone whispered.

The other man's footsteps fell silent. "Where?"

"Here," Longarm grunted, standing and snapping his Winchester to his shoulder.

He aimed quickly and fired. As William's forehead turned tomato red, Longarm's spent round smoked into the darkness over his shoulder, and he slid the Winchester to his left.

The rifle's bark echoed off the pines, and Hyatt gave a wheezing snarl as he dropped his weathered Springfield and splayed both hands across his chest, from which blood pumped—rich, red, and frothy with air bubbles.

Longarm drilled the man once more, sending him pinwheeling back into the trees as Dalia shouted, "*There*—get him, Jeff!"

Longarm bolted into the woods, leaping several deadfalls, then careening left toward the river. He stopped, hunkered down behind a mossy boulder, feeling the spray from the river to his left, and waited.

His left arm throbbed, and he could feel blood running out from under the bandage. He was chilled from the falling night but hot from exertion.

Running footsteps sounded—a heavy man running toward him.

Longarm stepped out from around the boulder. Jeff

saw him too late. The big man froze, and his dung-brown eyes widened in shock.

Longarm levered three rounds into the man's belly, then, hearing the thump of the heavy body hitting the ground, stepped back behind the boulder.

He waited. The river rushed and pounded. The night came down, leaving only a little gray in the sky between the canyon's craggy walls.

A dark figure appeared between him and the river. He waited until the woman had walked on past the boulder before he said, just loudly enough to be heard above the stream's roar, "It's over, Dalia. Toss away the rifle and turn around slow."

She froze. Her shoulders tensed. The last light glistened dully in the golden blond hair hanging straight down her back.

He knew what she was thinking.

"You don't want to die, Dalia."

She continued facing away from him. "Don't suppose you'd change your mind about South America, eh, Custis?"

"I reckon not."

She chuckled, her shoulders jerking slightly. "Then what would be the point of turning around slow?"

Longarm sighed. "I hear you."

She wheeled, swinging her rifle toward him.

Longarm closed his eyes and fired.

Watch for

**LONGARM AND THE
VAL VERDE MASSACRE**

the 367th novel in the exciting LONGARM
series from Jove

Coming in June!

GIANT-SIZED ADVENTURE FROM AVENGING ANGEL LONGARM.

BY TABOR EVANS

2006 Giant Edition:

LONGARM AND THE OUTLAW EMPRESS

2007 Giant Edition:

LONGARM AND THE GOLDEN EAGLE SHOOT-OUT

2008 Giant Edition:

LONGARM AND THE VALLEY OF SKULLS

penguin.com/actionwesterns